Black Library
Celebration
2022

After you enjoy the stories in this anthology,
we recommend the following titles:

WARHAMMER 40,000   WARHAMMER AGE OF SIGMAR   THE HORUS HERESY   WARHAMMER HORROR   WARHAMMER CRIME

Black Library
Celebration
2022

Mike Brooks, Marc Collins, Guy Haley,
Ray Cluley and C L Werner

BLACK LIBRARY

A BLACK LIBRARY PUBLICATION

'The Serpent's Dance' and 'The Shapers of Scars'
first published digitally in 2020.
'The Reaper's Gift' first published in *The Accursed* in 2021.
'No Use for Good Men' first published in *No Good Men* in 2020.
This edition published in Great Britain in 2022 by
Black Library, Games Workshop Ltd., Willow Road,
Nottingham, NG7 2WS, UK.

Represented by: Games Workshop Limited – Irish branch,
Unit 3, Lower Liffey Street, Dublin 1,
D01 K199, Ireland.

10 9 8 7 6 5 4 3 2 1

Produced by Games Workshop in Nottingham.
Cover illustration by Phil Moss.

See Black Library on the internet at

blacklibrary.com

Find out more about Games Workshop
and the world of Warhammer 40,000 at

games-workshop.com

Printed and bound by CPI Group (UK) Ltd, Croydon, CR0 4YY

Contents

The Serpent's Dance

Mike Brooks

Jovian security was just as alert as Amendera Kendel had expected. Every challenge was heavy with the potential for violence if it was not answered correctly; every automated check required the correct code to be transmitted at the correct moment, lest her ship be targeted by the massive gun barrels of orbital defence stations, or the weapons of the patrol fleet. Behind and beneath it all lurked the planet itself: a monstrous swirling eye, under whose baleful gaze everything was scrutinised.

Yet Amendera Kendel was not telling the truth, and still she was allowed to proceed.

'I don't like this,' she said flatly, watching the planet begin to loom up underneath them.

'Why?' Qelvyn Bura asked. The former soldier was cleaning the blade of her knife. 'You don't want to pull rank on them – there's no point trying to be subtle if you've already announced to the entire security system that the Regent's Agentia Tertius is approaching.'

'I *know* that,' Amendera replied testily. Qelvyn's attitude was generally irreverent at best, but she'd been with Amendera since Proxima Majoris, and Amendera trusted her. More than that, Qelvyn had seen Amendera unleash Exterminatus upon that world, and still stood with her. 'But if I had to resort to it, at least I'd have fewer fears about these defences being penetrated by hostile agents.'

The Warmaster was coming; that much was undeniable. At some point – tomorrow, next month, next year – the full force of his betrayal was going to strike towards Terra, but those commanding its defence knew better than to think the galaxy's greatest general would approach without laying the groundwork. The Jovian shipyards were essential to the war effort, and the planet's defences would be a fearsome bastion against any attacker… assuming they were not compromised. There had already been betrayals in the Sol System; who knew what others might lie in wait?

That was what Amendera was here to find out. Hopefully.

'You need to work on your charm,' Ruvier Dall commented. He was a quicksilver rogue – a trickster and conman who'd made a living playing the edges of the Imperium's rule, at the heart of its power. Qelvyn had found him in a penitentiary, and recruited him to be a part of Amendera's slowly forming team. Amendera hadn't understood why, until Qelvyn had pointed out that no one knew weak points like someone who exploited them. She'd also explained that no one liked laws and rules so much as the people who made a living by breaking them in ways that others could not, or did not dare. If everyone could do it, who would pay the criminal? The Imperium's stability and legislation suited people like Ruvier very well.

The uncertainty of a warzone, let alone the unthinkable aftermath of Horus' victory? Not so much.

'I'm not trying to be charming,' Amendera snapped.

'Well, you should start,' Ruvier told her. His face held the same easy smile regardless of what situation he was in, or who he was speaking to, and it ground at Amendera's nerves. 'You're supposed to be a noble.'

'You ever met any nobles?' Qelvyn asked him. 'I have. "Charming" is not exactly the word I'd use.'

'Not to people like us,' Ruvier conceded. 'But to other nobles…'

'I'm not a noble,' Amendera said softly. 'I'm a soldier, fighting a war she wasn't made for.' She wasn't sure if she was talking to Ruvier or herself. She might not have been born into a position of power, but she now held more of it than virtually any other human in the galaxy. She answered, theoretically, only to Malcador and the Emperor, and that was a worm that gnawed at her heart.

'None of us were made for this,' Ruvier said, and his voice was uncharacteristically sober, even if his smile remained. 'We'll just have to make the best of it.'

Jupiter's ruling elite lived on the polar Shoal city-stations: massive floating plates, within the gas giant's tenuous upper atmosphere but far enough from its gravity's grip not to be pulled into the thick, roiling clouds of hydrogen and helium below. The clan masters and mistresses of the enormous planet wielded great power, even now that the Sol System was increasingly ordered by the demands of Rogal Dorn, and they were privy to highly sensitive information.

They also, however, had not yet given up on their extravagant lifestyles. Exotic delicacies might be harder to source, and the sky above them might be lit up by the drive trails of patrol boats, but that was not enough to truly disrupt the Jovian social calendar. After all, it had been argued, was it not the first stage of defeat, to fear your enemy so much that you ceased to live as you wished? Dorn, who had torn down the Imperial Palace's glories in the name of defence, or walled them up inside adamantium, might have disagreed with that statement, but the void clans would not be denied. The Sapphire Ball was taking place over the next three days, and there would be no better opportunity to examine the collected nobility of Jupiter, and those guests who could still travel here, to see if any canker lurked within the jewel of the Sol System.

Qelvyn had suggested her own homeworld of Shenlong as Amendera's cover, but Amendera had refused, since the possibility of encountering someone who would know her story to be false was low, but not impossible. So it was that the noblewoman who strode into the grand hall of the Telenak clan was announced as Lady Voltar of the fictional planet Mollita, which, if questioned, Amendera would claim existed in the Segmentum Pacificus.

The sight that greeted her was almost enough to rob her once again of the speech she'd once foresworn.

The hall was enormous, and easily the largest chamber into which she'd set foot outside of the Imperial Palace itself. It was in shadow, punctuated with mirrored pillars that receded into the distance like the mighty trunks of a particularly regular, widely spaced forest, and the roof far above was of crystalflex, through which faint points of light could just be made out. Scattered here and there were artful rockeries so beautifully designed they almost appeared to be naturally occurring, with plants both taken from the biome of Terra and imported from the far reaches of the Imperium. Graceful automata in the shape of long-extinct ungulates stepped delicately on long, slender legs, broadcasting gentle music from pipes in their metallic antlers and bearing refreshment platters on their backs, while sporadic illumination was cast by hanging or free-floating clusters of lumens.

One of those floating lights drifted towards Amendera and took up station approximately a metre above her head. She looked up at it, then enquiringly at the major-domo standing to one side of the main doors.

'Please, your ladyship,' he said with a smile. 'It is merely to light your way.'

'This is going to make me nervous,' Qelvyn muttered as they moved off.

'It's going to make *you* nervous?' Ruvier replied quietly. 'I'm a criminal, I'm not used to being picked out like this.'

'Oh, and you think a soldier likes a giant glowing target following her around?'

'Quiet,' Amendera chided them softly. 'Keep your eyes open, and tell me what you see.'

They paused to subtly inspect the constellations around them. Each group had its own light: as Amendera watched, one would break away from another and drift towards a third, as nobles, governors and other wealthy or influential people finished exchanging pleasantries with one peer and began the process with another.

'You're going to have to get involved,' Ruvier said to her. 'First rule of a con is to look like you belong. Nobles always think people want to talk to them. And for the love of the Emperor, smile more – you're hard enough to like as it is.'

Amendera fingered the engraved torc around her neck. It had been a gift from Malcador, although it was far more tool than frippery, for it suppressed the null aura of a pariah. The emptiness that made others so desperately uncomfortable around her was diminished by it, but not removed: Qelvyn still said she felt uneasy, just rather less so. Amendera would need to counteract the effect of her pariah gene with charm, lest everyone avoid her, and their fact-finding mission come to nothing. It was a task more alien and more daunting than virtually any she had been set in her years serving the Somnus Citadel.

She took a deep breath, checked that the half-mask she wore on her upper face to obscure the aquila tattoo on her forehead was still in place, and headed for the nearest light.

Nobles, Amendera had found, were fond of using an abundance of words to say very little. It seemed almost wasteful to a soldier used to the concise clarity of battlemark, and even thoughtmark would not have been used in such garrulous fashion: there were no chatterers amongst the Sisters of Silence. After an hour, she was feeling as though she'd been buffeted by a turbulent river of inanities.

'Do these people not have a single thing of import to say?' she muttered in frustration, in the aftermath of the latest baron excusing himself from the circle of her illumination.

'You're paying attention to the wrong conversations,' Ruvier said from beside her. 'The opening words are a blind. It's tone of voice, posture, little mannerisms – that's how they're communicating. You're not responding to the right cues, so they don't know what to make of you – that's why they're not saying anything worthwhile.'

'And you can tell this how?' Amendera demanded. Ruvier shrugged.

'I've spent my life playing people. You were a soldier – if you walk into a firefight, I imagine you can tell at a glance who's where, who's shooting at who, where your allies are?'

'Yes,' Amendera said, somewhat offended. 'I'd be dead, otherwise.'

'That's how it is for me and people,' Ruvier said. 'There are times I've been dropped into a situation and had to decide instantly who my allies are, and whether to charge or take cover, if you'll pardon the analogy.'

'Perhaps I should have given you the role of noble,' Amendera muttered, shifting her shoulders. Fao and Kye, the twin dressers who were safely back on the ship, had made her a beautiful yet practical outfit based around a bodysuit that would allow her to kick someone in the head, with just enough flowing fabric in the right locations to make it look like she could not. She still felt uncomfortable and exposed in it, despite the concealed armour mesh, and would have vastly preferred something like the far more sober, utilitarian tunic and leggings worn by Qelvyn. Ruvier, on the other hand, would probably have been quite at home in fake finery. 'Qelvyn?'

'Everyone here has at least one bodyguard,' the Shenlongan replied. 'The usuals – discreet combat servitors, feral-world killers with behavioural implants, and I think I've seen a Lucifer Black. No obvious weapons, but if there aren't a dozen concealed blades in this room, then I'm a ratling.'

'How can you tell they're bodyguards if they don't have weapons?' Ruvier asked dubiously.

'The same way you can read the nobles,' Qelvyn replied. 'I understand people too, just in terms of who's likely to be hard to kill.' She took a sip of a strong, fragrant alcohol that was apparently distilled from Sigman plerries. 'No one's truly comfortable here, either – no one's moving far from their minders. *Except...*'

She turned towards Amendera, and took another sip of her drink while leaning closer. 'Over my right shoulder.

Blue-and-green robes, dark beard. He goes to speak with others, then returns to his little retinue after he's done – they don't go with him.'

Amendera focused on the man Qelvyn had indicated. He was tall and broad, and his bluffly handsome face held a naturally jovial expression. His beard was pointed and oiled, and his hair fell in soft waves past his shoulders.

'So why is he so much more comfortable than everyone else?' she wondered aloud. Sure enough, he was chatting merrily with the archduchess of Merillia – a round-faced woman with whom Amendera had spent an excruciating ten minutes talking about the impact of windblown ammonia crystals on the city-station's gravitic plates – while his two retainers stood under their light some distance away. 'Who is he?'

'According to this,' Ruvier said, consulting his data-slate, 'he's Durian Jarandille, merchant prince of somewhere I'm not even going to try to pronounce while I'm this sober. Aides are Kristanna Moristat and Jorud Gevaz.'

Amendera frowned. He didn't sound a likely candidate to be careless with his own safety, when others were so cautious. She tapped her chin thoughtfully.

The music filling the hall was becoming very slightly louder, and a few of the guests were starting to dance with each other between the mirrored columns. Amendera took a decision.

'I think we've achieved all we can with our initial approach,' she told the other two. 'I don't know how to talk to these people. Time to let the mask drop a little.'

'Are you sure?' Qelvyn asked uncertainly. 'That could get–'

'The next time we try subterfuge, I'm letting Ruvier lead,' Amendera said, cutting her off. 'For now, head-on is best. Stay here, and watch my back.'

She set off across the floor towards Jarandille with a far

more natural and purposeful gait than the largely aimless wandering she'd been doing until now, but she never got there. Kristanna Moristat – young, slim and dark-haired – stepped forward to intercept her, while Jorud Gevaz – taller and plumper, with a completely bald head – remained where he was, watching with only mild interest.

'Pardon me, milady,' Kristanna said, performing a curtsey. 'May I ask–'

'I intend to request a dance from Lord Durian,' Amendera told her briskly. She didn't know how to dance, but she didn't know how to make small talk either. Given a choice of the two, she'd take the one which involved movement: that, at least, she had not spent decades avoiding.

'Milady, Lord Durian is, as you can see, currently occupied,' Kristanna said. She kept her eyes lowered, and Amendera didn't think it was just out of respect for her supposed rank. Kristanna looked to be trembling a little. Fear of offending a noble? Or of something else?

If she was already on edge in some way, then unsettling her further might shake something loose.

'Well,' Amendera said, 'I intend to have a dance. Lord Durian may be occupied, but you are not.'

She reached out, took hold of Kristanna's wrist and shoulder, and swung her away.

Kristanna gasped and tried to resist, but Amendera was taller and stronger, and well versed in the physics of how bodies could be made to move in directions they did not wish to go. Even when deployed as a Silent Sister, she had on occasion needed to haul someone away for questioning: this was merely a variation on the theme, although it was true that she'd never interrogated someone to the lilting strains of wind instruments being played by automata.

She'd barely begun to pivot Kristanna towards a clear area of floor when a shock of recognition ran through her, and had her captive been paying attention, she likely could have wriggled free from Amendera's grasp. However, Amendera saw from the widening of Kristanna's eyes that she'd been struck by the same sensation.

'You're a blank,' Amendera muttered, recovering herself and sweeping Kristanna farther away from Jorud, who was looking on in apparent confusion.

'You're like me?' the other woman husked. 'I think? I didn't know... How...'

Kristanna's pariah influence wasn't large, or particularly strong. She would nullify psykana powers in her immediate area, but she didn't have anything close to the kind of void Amendera projected when her capabilities weren't being suppressed. When talking with other nobles, Durian would have been well outside the range of the natural unease Kristanna caused.

'What is your purpose here?' Amendera demanded. 'You shield him from psychic probes or attacks when he's with you, but stay away from him when he's socialising, so they don't take a dislike to him because of your aura?' Was Durian simply paranoid about his mind being invaded? In which case, why would he move away from Kristanna to talk with others? Or was he expecting a general psychic attack on the entire ball, of which he would have sufficient warning to hide behind his blank?

'Please, milady!' Kristanna begged, her eyes wide with alarm. 'I don't know what you mean!'

Amendera was no expert, but she knew that this was a place of honeyed smiles and sleek sentences, where words and glances could mean many things, or nothing at all. Kristanna was entirely too ill at ease, even for someone swept into a dance by an unknown noble. She had no smoothness, no guile; even her politeness was the product of fear, not experience. No dignitary would have such a person in their retinue.

Unless, of course, the dignitary was no such thing.

Amendera swung Kristanna behind a pillar, shielded from the view of their respective companions, and raised her hand to pull down her half-mask. She saw Kristanna's eyes travel up to the revealed aquila tattoo on her forehead, a common enough marking amongst the Silent Sisterhood. If Kristanna knew what it signified, which judging by the widening of her eyes, she did, then she would believe that Amendera's speech marked her as an oathbreaker.

An oathbreaker, like the renegade forces that had sworn themselves to the Warmaster. Amendera knew her vows had been changed rather than broken, no matter what certain of her former sisters might believe, but she had no compunction about using that perception to shake loose the tongue of someone who might be looking for such a kindred spirit.

'Tell me, Kristanna,' she said softly, catching the other woman's gaze and holding it. 'What is it that you are doing here?'

Kristanna's lip trembled for a moment, and then she spoke in a hurried, furtive rush. 'Milady, we must flee! We must get away – please, help me get away!'

Amendera frowned. 'Get away from where? And why?'

'From the *war!*' Kristanna urged, her expression clouded by fear. 'He is using me, and if you have turned your face from the Emperor then he will use you too! But we can escape!'

Of course we are used, Amendera wanted to tell her. *Our nature is our purpose.* And what life was there for a pariah, without purpose? Merely scorn, and solitude.

'Who is using you?' she asked instead, although she had already guessed the answer.

Kristanna looked back, as though to check the pillar was still between her and Lord Durian, which gave Amendera all she needed. She kept hold of Kristanna's hand and pulled the other woman after her, back the way they'd come.

Durian was now talking to Qelvyn and Ruvier, apparently in deep and earnest conversation. However, as Amendera approached she saw that Qelvyn's eyes had lost their sharpness, and Ruvier's face lacked his permanent smirk. Amendera reached up with her free hand, and removed her suppression torc.

She couldn't feel her null zone rolling out as her full aura was unleashed, but she could hear the murmurs of discomfort from the surrounding nobles as it reached them. Most notably, Durian turned towards her with a look of sick horror, and Qelvyn and Ruvier seemed to snap out of a trance.

'Lord Durian' wasn't expecting a psychic attack; he was a psyker himself, and he had been manipulating the minds of some of the most influential people in the Sol System.

He recovered well: far more quickly than most that Amendera had faced, but then he'd been moving in and out of a blank's aura in any case. He lunged at her, all pretence gone, seeking to achieve with physical force what he had no hope of managing through his warp-tainted gifts. However, Amendera had been training in combat since before she was fully grown.

She punched him in the throat.

Her knuckles met his larynx with a sickening crunch. He staggered backwards, hands flying uselessly to his neck, and Qelvyn swept his legs out from under him. Durian fell backwards and landed hard on the floor; Amendera reached out and caught Qelvyn's wrist before the knife that had suddenly appeared in her hand could bury itself in the psyker's chest.

'He will need to be questioned,' she told her armswoman, looking down at the helpless, wheezing man. The brief scuffle had drawn shocked gasps, and the major-domo was hurrying over, but Amendera had no time for the sensibilities of the nobility. 'What were you doing here?' she demanded of Kristanna, whose eyes were wide. 'What was the purpose?'

'Milady, I don't know!' Kristanna began to sob. 'Durian was to speak to others, and I was to be his cover so he was not detected as a psyker, that is all I know...'

'Lady Voltar!' the major-domo cried as he approached, four armed guards at his back. 'Lady Voltar, I–'

Amendera saw when he entered her aura, as his expression of alarm and outrage shifted to include disgust as well. She stepped forward, to put him on the back foot: her untouchable nature meant she would never be liked, but it had the advantage that people were more likely to agree with her just to make her go away.

These days, of course, she theoretically had no need of any such advantage, but she would take what she could get.

'I am an agent of the Sigillite,' she said bluntly, stripping off her left glove and holding up her hand so the metallic scars on her palm were visible to him. 'This man is a witch and an imposter – he is currently subdued, but no one who has been in conversation with him is to leave this hall until they have been examined for psychic influence.'

'Lady Voltar, that is impossible!' the major-domo protested. 'It is beyond my authority to–'

'I have just commanded it, so that is no longer the case,'

Amendera said, interrupting him. 'You have guards with guns – ensure it happens, or you will answer to the Regent's displeasure.'

The major-domo swallowed visibly, but looked again at Malcador's mark on her palm, and managed a shaky nod.

Kristanna tugged at Amendera's arm with a sudden cry of alarm. 'Jorud! Where did Jorud go?'

Amendera glanced at Qelvyn and Ruvier, who shook their heads.

'Sorry, milady,' Ruvier said, sounding contrite for once, and not a little shaken. 'This bastard had his fingers in my brain, I didn't see–'

'That way,' Qelvyn said, pointing towards a door in the far wall of the huge hall. 'I'm sure he went that way.'

'He is the dangerous one,' Kristanna hissed at Amendera. 'Jorud!'

'Not Durian?' Amendera looked down again at the psyker, but the desperation in Kristanna's voice held its own truth. Amendera was used to hunting rogue witches, people who had trampled over the laws of humanity and reality in the service of their own interests. She'd assumed, once he had been revealed, that Durian was behind whatever scheme they'd uncovered here.

Perhaps he too was merely a tool.

She shoved Kristanna at Qelvyn. 'This girl is a blank, so she'll keep Durian suppressed. Get what answers you can from them. If either gives you any trouble, kill them both. Him first.' She turned to the major-domo. 'What is beyond those doors?'

The major-domo seemed to have recognised that she held authority over him, for his reply was prompt. 'Many things, milady, but it is possible to access the chambers of the High Thane.'

Amendera cursed. 'Then you may have an intruder.' She began to run towards the door.

'Lady, should I call for reinforcements?' the major-domo shouted after her.

'No need!' Amendera replied. She touched the micro-bead in her ear, activating a vox transmission to the ship on which she'd arrived. 'Come with all speed.'

The time for subtlety was over.

The two guards on the other side of the door were dead, each killed by the slash of a powerblade that had cut through their beautifully engraved gorgets. Amendera took in the sight with the dispassionate expertise of a seasoned killer: the right-hand guard had fallen backwards from the force of a backhanded blow; the other had lunged for Jorud, who had... ducked? Slipped behind the guard, opened his throat, snatched his shotgun, and pushed him forwards to die. Which meant Jorud had gone left. And yes, there was a short trail of dark ash, as the guards' blood had flash-dried on the power knife that had ended their lives, then flaked off it.

Amendera prised the other guard's shotgun loose from their dead fingers, and tucked their combat blade into the sash around her waist for good measure. She had a concealed boot-blade, but there was no sense in not taking these weapons now that the time for subtlety was over. Nothing she had available was as familiar as the great, two-handed sword she'd wielded as an Oblivion Knight, but she would have to make do.

She moved quickly but cautiously, slipping past reinforced crystalflex panels that looked out over the great bulge of Jupiter below, so large that its horizon barely curved, even at this altitude. There were no servants around, but these were clearly service areas: they lacked the ostentatiousness of the corridors Amendera had been ushered through on the way to the grand hall, with their gilded frescoes and towering works of hololithic art. This part of the complex was where the food was made, the laundry was washed, the accounts were run, and all the other myriad tasks that allowed the Jovian high clans to live in such effortless, unthinking luxury. It would also cut between different areas of the palace, ensuring that the menials could come and go without polluting the hallways of their betters.

The boom of a shotgun reverberated through the corridors, quickly followed by shouts. Amendera hastened her pace, cutting right at the next junction. Here was a servant, in a pool of his own blood and half-propped against the wall where he'd fallen. A shotgun fired again, closer now: Amendera stepped past the dying man, and went around the next turn with her weapon raised.

She came out into a larger hall, where corridors met and stairs ran up to another level. Jorud Gevaz was standing over another dead man in servant's livery: he whirled towards her, raising his stolen gun, and Amendera dived forwards into a roll. The shot missed her, and she came up onto one knee, braced her own weapon against her shoulder, and pulled the trigger.

The weapon's kick pulled her aim off, and her return shot flew wide to shatter part of the stone bannister of the stairs beyond Gevaz. He fired again, but Amendera knew better than to remain in one spot, and was already up and darting to her left. She changed direction as he swung his weapon's muzzle towards her once more; the disturbance in the air caused by that shell's passage kissed her cheek, and then she was on him before he could fire again.

Gevaz swung the stock of his gun at her head, wielding it in both hands like a short staff, but Amendera blocked it with her left arm and aimed her shotgun at his body with her right. It was a bulky weapon, and Gevaz smashed his own left arm down into the gun's barrel before she could bring it properly to bear. The impact caused her to discharge the next shell into the floor, throwing up sparks, so Amendera dropped it, grabbed the barrel of Gevaz's shotgun with her left hand to force it upwards, and drew the combat blade from her sash with her right. He knocked her first stab at his face wide and kicked at her left knee, sending a jolt of pain through it, but she didn't fall.

'Malcador has sent you to your death,' Gevaz hissed, seizing the wrist of her knife arm. Perhaps he hoped his words would intimidate or shake her, but Amendera Kendel had accepted the possibility of death in service long before she'd ever taken the Oath of Tranquillity. If Terra needed her life, she would give it unquestioningly.

She let go of his shotgun and stepped in before he could react, slamming her left elbow into his cheek and then clamping her arm down on his to trap it in place with the gun pointing uselessly past her. He staggered and she followed, looking to pin him against the wall behind him, but he shifted his weight towards her left and her knee buckled slightly, allowing him to spin her around.

He slammed his head forwards, and Amendera's face exploded into pain as her nose snapped with the sharp *crack* of breaking cartilage. Eyes watering and half-blinded, she lashed out with her good knee and felt it connect. Gevaz doubled over, the breath blasted from his body, and she felt his grip on her knife hand slacken slightly. She twisted, trying to free it and blink her eyes clear of involuntary tears–

'Intruders detected. Eliminating...'

The mechanical voice from behind Gevaz was accompanied by the whine of a rapid-charging melta weapon. The heretic launched himself to his right, releasing Amendera's wrist and abandoning his shotgun to be trapped under her arm, and leaving Amendera in the sights of the two Crusader-class guardian automata who had clearly responded to the commotion. She leaped the other way from him, pursued by a thermal bloom as the air where she'd just been standing was superheated.

Both insectoid robots pivoted to follow her movement, perhaps because she was the only one with an obvious weapon. Amendera managed to juggle the shotgun into her grasp and fired a snap shot, but the solid slug only left a dent in the foremost automaton's carapace. Both meltas were powering up again. Amendera tensed, trying to pick the right moment to dodge or duck, and well aware that it would likely be futile.

The distinctive *crump-roar* of bolter shells filled the air, and the rearmost Crusader came apart under remorseless and deadly accurate fire. Its companion turned like a hunting beast, ready to eliminate this higher priority threat, but its meltagun was obliterated before it could fire, and its cranial unit followed a moment later.

Helig Gallor strode through the smoke and twisted metal in the unmarked grey power armour of Malcador's chosen. The former Death Guard had been waiting on Amendera's ship in case of emergencies, for an Astartes warrior would have not gone unremarked even in such cosmopolitan company as had been present in the grand hall. Amendera suspected that given the speed of his arrival, there were now fewer intact doors within the palace than there had been.

Gallor turned his helm towards Jorud Gevaz and raised his bolter. Gevaz smiled at him.

'Hydra Dominatus.'

Amendera saw him press his palm to his ornate belt buckle a moment before Gallor pulled the trigger. The traitor's head and upper body disappeared as the bolter shell obliterated flesh and bone, but the roar of that shot was followed by a judder in the floor, and the faint boom of something that sounded almost like an echo of it, but was not.

Amendera looked upwards instinctively, as though she could see through the ceiling towards the stars. 'Were those shots? A bombardment?' Surely the Warmaster couldn't have arrived while they'd been here?

'No,' Gallor replied, with the certainty of a warrior who not only had enhanced senses, but had also witnessed many bombardments in his existence. 'Multiple simultaneous detonations. Explosive charges.'

An emptiness opened up inside Amendera's stomach. 'The great hall. Now!'

Not everyone in the grand hall had died when Gevaz had activated his remote detonator, but roughly two-thirds had: all of them held there under Amendera's personal order. Jovian security had clearly suspected that she'd been involved with the scheme in some way by corralling the guests, but Amendera had turned her quiet fury on them. When it came down to it, they hadn't dared stand against the authority of the Sigillite, especially not when it was backed by a grey-armoured Astartes. Amendera had left unmolested, with the knowledge that she was no traitor.

Merely a failure.

She stared down at the shredded body of Ruvier Dall while

rage lashed around inside her, seeking an outlet. The explosives had been concealed in the deer automata, and their shattered metallic bodies had reaped a heavy toll.

'Why try to get to the High Thane, then?' she asked quietly.

'A decoy? Multiple targets? Perhaps this was a backup, should that attempt fail,' Gallor rumbled. 'This was the work of the Twentieth. With them, there is always more in play than can be seen.'

'But the High Thane still lives,' Qelvyn pointed out, prodding at the dressing on her ribs and right arm. 'So there's that.' The blast had killed Kristanna, and Qelvyn had executed Durian while the first blood of her own shrapnel injuries had been staining her clothes, before the psyker could threaten them. The trail had gone cold before Amendera had had a chance to start following it.

'This is a war that I don't know how to fight,' Amendera said. The admission removed no weight from her soul; instead it seemed to crush her a little more.

'I believe the war that is coming will be the same for us all,' Gallor said. 'This is just one aspect of it. We must endure.'

'Easy for you to say,' Qelvyn told him. 'The rest of us aren't like you.'

Amendera took a breath and closed her eyes, looking inwards for the peace of tranquillity. She had left the oath of the Silent Sisterhood behind her, but the discipline still remained.

This task, this duty, is greater than I can comprehend. And yet I will attempt it, for this is now my purpose. To abandon it would be to have abandoned my Sisterhood for nothing. This is the task the Emperor has set me.

I am not Astartes, but I too will endure. I will make this battlefield my own.

She opened her eyes again. There were lines of attack: the source of the automata, the compromised security protocols that had allowed them into the palace, the manufacture of Gevaz's belt detonator… All things that might lead back to the minds behind this. Perhaps this was yet another distraction; perhaps by following these trails, she was taking her eye off another, more pressing threat. Yet she could not stand still and do nothing, waiting wide-eyed for the real enemy to show its face in its own time.

'We have work to do.'

YOUR
NEXT READ

HORUS RISING
by Dan Abnett

After thousands of years of expansion and conquest, the human Imperium is at its height. His dream for humanity accomplished, the Emperor hands over the reins of power to his Warmaster, Horus, and heads back to Terra.

The Shapers of Scars

Marc Collins

'Three things shape a man's scars: the foe, time, and the healer's rites.'

– Fenrisian proverb

The old woman sits in the chill of the apothecarion, but she does not feel the bite of the cold. Long ago she passed beyond such things, in the way that only a life lived beneath slate-grey skies with the scent of salt and ice as constant companion can bless her with. She realises, on some soul-deep level, that she carries the world of her birth with her. Bound to her as surely as an oath. She sits, and she watches, and she waits. She is the eye of the storm, a rare ocean of calm, as others hustle and rush about her.

Before them a queen lies dying.

The old woman, the *gothi*, Bodil, spares her queen a look. A glance of recognition. A nod of respect. Her long pale fingers close around a bone tile, and she raises it to her face, pinning the fates in place, bound by rite. Worn gums draw back from her teeth, her pallid skin crinkles around scars and tattoos; she does not hide her age, nor the weight that this undertaking places upon her. Her blue eyes focus, pale as spring ice, as she reads the tile and curses.

'Skitja!'

One of the medicae thralls lets his eyes drift to her, giving her an askance look. She laughs, and bares her teeth.

'Oh, do I offend your sensibilities? If you have not the patience for me then get away from her! I would not trust half of you to calve a grox, let alone minister to our jarl!' The thrall's jaw flaps, noiselessly. Bodil snorts as she leans forward to look again at her queen.

At Katla Helvintr.

The jarl's eyes, those sea-storm-blue eyes – a huntress' eyes – are closed, locked so by the balms of the medicae and the venoms of the beast. Her auburn hair, like a crown of fire and glory, is matted with blood and sweat where it is not seared away by the acid's bite. In her weakness, she has never looked more mighty. More deserving of ascension to the Allfather's side.

She is called jarl, for she has carved out a hall and a hearth amidst the stars, as her line has for generations. She is called the Huntress Queen, for she has harried the enemies of the Allfather from their lairs, and made trophies of them. Here in the cold light of the apothecarion, Bodil thinks of such things with a wry smile. She cannot see the mighty void-ivory that adorns much of the ship, but knowing it is there is a comfort. And comfort is needed here today, as she casts the runes over the nicked thread of a valiant warrior.

'If you die, my queen,' the old woman says almost idly, 'then the halls of the slain shall be the lesser for your lack. We each carry our red snow with us, for it is cold in the shadow of Morkai, is it not? Perhaps that is why they raised their mountain so high, the Sky Warriors, that they might ever be in His light.' She laughs, dry and cracked. Forced. She shakes her head. 'But what would I know? I am only the gothi.'

Bodil checks the runes again, and scowls as she snaps up the tiles and drums them against the steel table she leans over. 'It will be close, this thing,' she whispers. 'She is strong, but there are few stronger than the pull of their *wyrd*.' She shakes her head. 'The wyrm is her fate. It will cut her thread one day, perhaps not this day…'

Her eyes drift to the knife that sits beside the worn leather pouch of runes, gleaming alongside the long, thin needles of bone and the bowls of pigment. She does not reach for it. She will not countenance it as inevitable.

'It will be the wyrm that ends her, but it is the hand of a loved one that will take her life. Not in betrayal, but with love.'

And through it all, Katla sleeps. She stirs fitfully, with the slow bite of pain. Venom and acid claw at her, gnawing at mind and muscle. She twitches, every breath forced from her through the iron ministrations of machines and the tubes which crowd her throat.

Katla suffers, and she dreams.

'I want it found,' Katla hisses. 'The beast is near. I can all but smell it. Bring us about. Weapons readied. It cannot have got far.' She sits upon the edge of her command throne, watching the silent void pass by as a tumble of rock and ice intrudes, but it does not dominate her attention. Her eyes are always in motion. Always seeking advantage against her enemies. She runs a hand through her hair, before checking again that she is still armed – that she is ready.

Twin axes are sheathed at her hips. Simple and direct. They have no names. Along the back of the throne lies her spear, its length gilded and marked with the runes of the world of Winter and War. It is called Fimbulgeir. It sits as a symbol of her authority, as a crystallisation of what it means to be jarl, to bear her Warrant of Trade. To stand as a queen.

Not of a ship, or a people, but as a symbol of something greater.

It has been many years since Katla claimed the rule of the Davamir Compact, ascended as queen amongst her peers in the other dynasties. It is a fleeting honour, and in time it will pass to another name. The dour and warlike Lamertines, perhaps. Or the addled ranks of the Radrexxus.

'Spare me,' she mutters, 'from the joyless and the joy-curdled.'

'Jarl?' asks a voice from an augur-station, and she waves it off with a smile.

'Nothing,' she says, and stands. She stretches, muscles flexing with the need of the hunt. It is primal, this urge. It has kept mankind fed and safe, and standing between the teeming masses and the hungry dark. Where there have been beasts, there have been hunters. That is the lesson of Fenris. The wisdom her ancestors carried to the stars, and enshrined in the iron bones of her vessel, the Wyrmslayer Queen.

'No auspex returns,' the voice says again. This time she looks at the master of the auspex station. He is young. Eager. He is called Svend. She knows every man and woman upon her bridge. She knows, and understands, and judges. 'They said it would be here. One last hive ship wounded and alone. Damn the Navy, and their–'

'Peace, Svend,' she laughs. 'They will not have robbed us of glory. Its spoor is on the wind. It will give itself away before ever we have to search for it.'

'How can you be sure, jarl?' He asks the question innocently. She wonders if she was ever so starved for knowledge and experience, in her father's time of rule.

32

'I know,' she says. 'How often have we hunted together, Svend? I have led the wild hunt across the Allfather's dominions for decades without rest, before ever you came into my service.'

The man bows his head, and looks away. She does not mean to shame him, but it is unavoidable. As certain as bloodshed.

'I want my prize,' she says, to a chorus of affirmations.

They will not fail her. The very thought of it is poison.

She looks away, just in time to see something flicker in the darkness of the abyss. Something moves amidst the ice and rock, its movements slow and languid in one moment – before it springs to sudden, writhing life.

A monstrous thing of chitin and muscle, and animal rage. The Imperial Navy had fought it, harried it from its fellows, wounded it. Yet now the beast returns, its fury kindled.

'There it is,' she says, and grins. 'Did I not tell you? The void speaks to me. It speaks to all of the blood Helvintr. The Emperor's hunters.' She laughs. 'Bring us around. Show it our teeth.'

The engines strain against the darkness and the cold, burning hot as the blood of worlds. Below them the gun-crews are about their work – readying the vessel's great killing implements. Shells slide home and the macrocannons seal and arm with peals of vast thunder. Lance batteries crackle with bound fury. Great void-harpoons ratchet into place, they bare them like fangs. The older, bestial name for such implements has been long lost to them, but the claws will find their mark regardless.

'Fire!' she roars. The guns cut across the void with light and a fury that echoes her own as the blackness is streaked by sudden flame. Red against the darkness. For a moment they can see every detail of the creature – its ice-rimed hide and questing tendrils. Maws glimmering wetly, edged with razor teeth. Detonations blossom from its skin as it forges on, plunging, diving, jaws yawning in the eternal silence of the night.

The first boarding spores are already racing towards the ship, behind the questing nest of feeder tendrils. The thing has the audacity to think itself a predator.

But beneath the eye of the Wyrmslayer Queen *it can be nothing more than prey.*

Katla bucks and writhes upon the table as phantom pain racks her. Her ship was violated, then her flesh, and she remembers. She relives it, moment by moment, even as Bodil watches and the surgeons pore over their charge. There are more tubes now, and the relentless motion of knives. They are opening her, as surely as any action of the enemy. Bodil leans closer, sniffs the air.

'She cannot be allowed to die,' she whispers. The medicae do not look to her, set upon their task. 'It is more than her body that must be healed, it is her spirit. She must be braced in her soul, rune-marked and warded.' She reaches for the first needle, testing its weight as though judging its soul. 'They will claw at you, my queen, these wights of the Underverse. They wish to pull you down beneath the thick ice, amongst the dead ships and drowned men. Yet even spirits may be made to fear.'

She takes the needle, and gently dips it into the first of the pigments, smearing its end black. She moves, and the medicae flinch away from her. They see her as a spectre in her own right, something ghoulish that has no place in a realm of healing.

She ignores them all as she brings the needle to skin, and begins to tap the ink into her queen's wounded skin. Katla bucks and shudders, her body convulsing at the violation. Bodil places one gnarled hand on Katla's shoulder, forcing her down against the table.

'This is not where you die, my queen,' she whispers. The

medicae work faster at her words, spurred on to test their magic against hers. 'I will ensure that you are strong.'

There are so many. She has long since lost count. The auspex dings and whirls with their onslaught. Pods, missiles, spores that bear living ruin and plasmic destruction.

She laughs from her high seat, and thinks her hall inviolate. The ship rings, sings, sighs, screams with alarm and siren. 'Örlendr!' someone cries. Alien! Their iron skin has been ruptured and breached, the minions of the enemy swarm upon them and within them. Somewhere, someone has sent up the signal, or the ship's own bellicose machine-spirit has scented their spoor.

'Spears!' she cries. The ship responds. The crew move at their stations, swift as prowling beasts. The Queen comes about, shows the monster her flank, and fires.

The great harpoons cross the gap, almost faster than the eye can follow but thrown with a hunter's precision, driving themselves into the beast's great thorax. Ichor stains the void in great boiling gouts. Kaleidoscopic bursts of alien chemicals, spurting into the war-scarred void. It struggles and squirms, suddenly and brutally aware of its own wounding, of its binding. Tight as any bond from story or legend, a chain made of the impossible. To cage abominations, and leave them readied for the killing blow.

It lashes out, and a great feeder tendril scours its way across the Queen's rune-marked hull. Air rushes from it like blood, and the entire ship shakes. Katla grasps at her throne, cursing even through her savage grin.

This is what it means to be a queen.

They are locked together. Ship and kraken, man and beast. The harpoons wind on their chains, drawing it ever closer. Still they wrack it with fire, carving into it as though it were already dead. Merely meat. Yet it struggles, and thrashes. Prey never truly comprehends its fate. There is always the dream of escape; even the lowest of beasts understands that. If they can merely fight, or chew through a limb, then there is hope.

Hope is the first casualty of the hunt. It is what must be stripped from the prey.

Fire whips across the beast's flanks again, sending it into another fit of savage convulsions. Parasite vanguard organisms stir across its plates, close enough now that they can hurl themselves at the iron ramparts of the ship. Countless of them are annihilated against the void shields, or burst apart under the attentions of point defence cannons.

Some make it through, some always make it through. That is the allure of warfare, the song that has kept mankind sharp as spear points down the long millennia of its rule.

'With me!' she cries, and the crew look to her with fearful longing. Her huscarls peel from the chamber's edges, flowing into place around her – as smoothly as armour clicking into place. 'There are beasts below!' she insists, a heady grin upon her face. Her joy is infectious. Her second, Eirik, smiles back.

'They are no match for us, jarl!'

'Let us hope not,' she laughs. 'We have yet to find a beast or monster that is a match for the Helvintr!'

She pauses at the great doorway of the bridge, and turns to regard her warriors and her crew.

'My friends, we have hunted the length and breadth of the Imperium, chasing the rumours of sailors and the reports of the Navy. We ride where others dare not, and fight those things that lesser men would shirk from facing, do we not?' They cheer with her. Fists pound at console casings, upon breastplates, against shields. 'You are my chosen! The Allfather's favoured! Always seeking the most glorious of prey! The most deadly of hunts! All for these moments, when victory lies upon the blade's edge!'

Beyond the viewscreens, the beast struggles in their grasp, lashing out with all the wounded fury it can muster. If they do not act soon, though, it will be the poison in their veins that undoes them.

'With me!' she cries, and they share her savage joy. They almost rush to outpace her, but she turns them back with a grin and the flat of the spear – reminding them of place and primacy. There can be no mistakes in facing an enemy such as this.

A tide of snapping, screeching bodies. The rushing puppet-horde of the hive mind. To test themselves against such an army, to best them on the field of battle – even if that field was bounded by iron, and the uncaring void…

She thinks of these things, and they do not slow her. If anything, her progress into the deeps of the ship is all the quicker, all the more yearning.

The work is intricate, delicate. Bodil marks her queen again and again, blood and ink running down the ruin that has become half of her face. She smooths away the layers of fluid, revealing the work beneath as the needle taps and probes and shapes. Others may come after, with their clever knotwork and steadier hands – but it is she who has marked her queen, and made her. She works runes into the art, signs of binding and deliverance. Marks of aversion, and assurances of oaths.

'When they see you, they will think that you are a talisman come to life to be so rune-marked.' The old woman laughs as she speaks.

The medicae give her *such looks*. This is, after all, their domain, and she is an intruder. They understand, but they fear. A gothi is a figure of the spirits, and the whisper of the Underverse, and perhaps they are afraid that she is here to see their jarl's spirit off. Perhaps it is because she speaks, even if her charge cannot hear her.

'And perhaps you are, my queen, perhaps you are a talisman. Symbols are stronger than men, and they cut sharper than a blade.'

The slumbering jarl does not stir. The drugs and unguents of the healers are strong, just as the one they must subdue. The work of the medicae is thorough and methodical, stemming her bleeding and bracing bones. Paring away the skin that is too ravaged to save. She is a ruin, and they are restoring her as ably as any shipwright would restore a vessel. Surgery is a battlefield all its own, where there are inevitably casualties.

'Sleep, my queen,' Bodil whispers. 'Sleep, and dream of the glory that you have won, and of the glories yet to come. There is an Imperium waiting for you, beyond your bed of blood and memories.'

The lesser beasts die in their droves, hewn apart by gunfire and blade. Katla strides into the heart of it, her spear tearing through chitin with every swing and thrust. They are everywhere, in such numbers that there is no need to aim. They are a crimson wave of motion – hooves and bladed limbs stamp and stab at the decking, jaws thrash with needle fangs or flailing nests of tendrils.

She does not care about their monstrous variety. They are prey!

'Into them!' she screams, and her warriors charge. Every battle is a vindication. Pride in her men, in her culture, in her rule. It is not a soulless pursuit as the Lamertines might have it. Nor the pretentious flailing of a Radrexxus war effort. It is beautiful – war as it should be, sanctified in the Allfather's sight. Men throw themselves forward, mail clinking over their void-armour. Axes and swords clatter against shields, even as blasts from laslocks cut across the corridor. The first wave of monstrosities goes down in a rush of ichor and fragments of bursting plate. The lesser monstrosities are easy prey, no real challenge for her warriors.

They have fought such things before. In the void and upon savage worlds beyond count. The hive fleet's spoor are amongst their favourite prey, but they have fought the savage greenskins and the duplicitous aeldari, and a dozen joyless human cultures with the same bladed enthusiasm as they bring to this battle.

Katla casts Fimbulgeir across the field of battle, and watches as it impales a brain-bloated psyker beast. The thing's whipping tail flails in the air, and the deck rimes itself with ice as it loses control of its power. Fire bleeds along the wound, and the thing bursts with a shriek of resonant psy-feedback. Katla cheers, and her men bellow their approval.

'The spear is cast!' she howls, drawing her axes. The weight of them is reassuring, their black blades grinning like old friends. She hacks at whatever gaunts dare to come near, their charge already rendered erratic without the guiding light of their synapse beast.

The snapping creatures throw themselves against the shields, only to be beaten down. Axe blades open skulls, puncture throats, gouge out eyes. They are cast down like the chaff they are. Slowly, the line of men pushes onwards. One of the beasts turns, a warrior-form, and fires. Acid and writhing maggot-like projectiles slap heavily against the face of one of her huscarls, and the man falls. Screaming, clawing at his face. She spits to one side. It is no fate for a warrior. She holsters an axe, and draws her sidearm – her glory. Wrathspitter. It is ancient, a relic of a bygone age. Even as a pistol, a volkite is potent. One of the greatest instruments of destruction ever constructed by mankind's forgotten weaponsmiths. She fires, and the warrior-form ceases to be. It detonates, caught for a moment in the deflagrating power of the beam.

Her warriors surge forward, eager for their own revenge. Claws meet blades, or bury themselves in shields. She takes up her axes again, swinging one in each hand as she fights her way towards her spear with a flurry of strikes. Replacing the axes with the spear, once more, thrusting through another screeching maw in a burst of ichor.

She is complete. The huntress queen.

The decking shakes, as though to challenge the legend they are crafting. The source of the noise surges, faster than it has any right to move, through the ranks of lesser beings. They bristle, muscles bunching more readily, focus colouring their glaring dead eyes. It is vast, a king of monsters – a thing bred as a living siege engine. Its plate is thick. Its weapons mighty. Vents upon its back spew toxic vapours, and acid oozes from swollen cyst-nodes. It shudders, and gouts a great stream of acid into their ranks.

Katla dives to one side. Others are not as swift. She hears screams, and scents the chemically cooking flesh. She roars her hate at the monster before her. She hurls herself into the fray.

'Hold her!' Bodil screams, and the medicae obey without thinking, rushing to their jarl's aid. When a spirit-talker commands, you listen. Their hands hold Katla to the steel of the table, even as the needle bites her skin once more. Bodil draws back, sucking her breath in through her teeth, her focus absolute. 'Her spirit is strong. See how she fights? She will fight forever, that one. When they try to cut her thread, she will fight and they will wish they had never made the attempt.' She reaches for the bag of runes once more, picks it up, and shakes it experimentally.

Everything stinks of blood and cauterised flesh. She casts the runes to the table with a clatter, and allows herself to move from her queen's side. 'Hmm…' she whispers; her fingers gnarl around one of the tiles, and she allows herself the faintest of smiles. 'That's better.'

* * *

It lumbers forward, and she moves to meet it. It is slow, and she is swift. A great scythe of bone sweeps over her head, so close that she can feel the rush of displaced air. She thrusts her spear up, the powered blade gouging into the thing's flank. She laughs at it, almost face to face with the alien monstrosity.

Las-fire and solid shot impacts along its armoured bulk, and it writhes in the rain of ordnance. Another great weapon-limb shudders, spasms, and vomits liquid death into their ranks. Her huscarls try to hide behind their shields, or raise their weapons in meek acts of aversion. It does nothing. Their skin bubbles, boils, sloughs away. They cease to be men, reduced to mere pools of flesh and shattered bones.

The bladed limb swings around again, catching her hard across her armoured chestplate. She spits blood, and reaches for her axes. The spear is lodged in the monster's side. She grits her teeth, lashes out again. Her blades find one of the heaving, tumorous poison sacs, hooking at it, slashing until it bursts. The beast rears back, screeching in alien agony. The rush of acid and ichorous blood washes over her, drowning her left side in the searing wrath of the monster. The vengeance of the monster is calculated, a trap for her hunter's ways. She drove for the heart, and that heart has proven to be bitter between her teeth. She drops the axe in her left hand, fingers opening and closing as the agony washes over her.

Other spears find it now, cast from amongst the ranks of her faithful. It whips around to face them, screaming even as her remaining axe slams into its side. Again, and again. Bullets and spears transfix it, but the last thing it will know – what she will carve upon its very flesh – is that it was the jarl of Helvintr who will end it.

She is still striking, still clawing at it, when it tumbles to the ground, and consciousness finally fails her, and bears her down with it.

* * *

The first breath that returns to her is a long, gasping one. Katla practically throws herself up from the steel bench on which she reclines. Her fingers claw at the metal, and she writhes like a pinned beast. Her eyes are wild, and she feels pain radiate through every facet of her being. The medicae bay is almost empty, devoid of the practitioners of the art of healing.

She flinches.

'Ah, my queen.' The voice is weary, tired and worn down by constant effort, and by worry. The old gothi looks at her, reverent and adoring. 'They did not think that you would survive, but they are merely priests of the flesh. What do they know of such things?'

'I live?' Katla asks unsteadily, and the old woman simply laughs.

'Of course you live, my queen! This would be a poor Underverse, the merest echo of the eternal. A fine ship, but a poor hall in which to dwell.'

'My men?'

'Many were lost to the ravages of the wyrm, but our strength endures. Eirik lives. He is strong, that one, you ought to take heed of that more. You are not alone, in all this.'

'No,' Katla says, with a small smile. Even that motion is full of pain. 'I have you.'

'Always, my queen.' Bodil nods. 'They have worked upon your flesh, while I girded your soul.' She reaches out, picks up the gleaming glass of a mirror. 'Would you like to see, my queen, what you have become?'

Katla takes the glass. Most of her auburn hair is gone. Her left side is a pitted, scarred ruin. Counterseptics and alkali still streaks her, along with the ink and blood of her remaking. She has *become*, under Bodil's art, and healer's rites. The ink flows and dances across the scarring, the left side of her face rendered into the snarl of a lupine skull. It is beautiful work, etched with love, and all the skill that desperation's fugue can impart. It is void-black, and yet riven through with gold and ochre. Bronze glimmers upon her skin as intricate and sacred as any electoo of the Iron Priesthoods. The winding knotwork covers the scars – drowning them in the bestial half-mask of Bodil's devotion. There are runes etched there. Oaths, too. The eye of the wolf, the lightning of the Allfather's unity. They are marked into her very skin. Burned into her soul.

She has become a promise.

'Well?' Bodil asks. She bows her head, and does not look at her queen, her jarl.

Katla stares at the mirror, letting her eyes drift across every detail of her rebirth. Many others would shirk from such a thing. It would drive a lesser man mad. Katla does not wish to howl, or beat at the walls. She will not break upon fate's anvil. She will shape it, as she is shaped by it, and so she takes the only course left to her. The only thing she can do.

Katla Helvintr smiles.

YOUR
NEXT READ

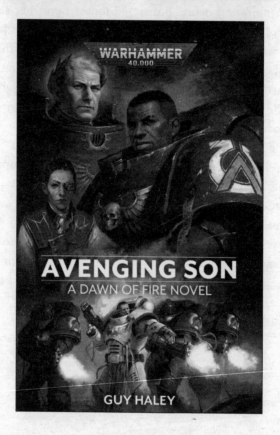

AVENGING SON
by Guy Haley

As the Indomitus Crusade spreads out across the galaxy, one battlefleet must face a dread Slaughter Host of Chaos. Their success or failure may define the very future of the crusade – and the Imperium.

WARHAMMER™
CRIME

No Use for Good Men

Guy Haley

DECRYPTING
>>>>*Incoming vox-script message*
>>>>*Originator Probator (First Class) Fyedor Blovast, ident 032567AZ#-Princus, Lex district Nearsteel (sub-area Inner/Outer rings)*
>>>>*Intended recipient Chief Justicius Maskell Resk, Lex district Nearsteel (greater designation)*
>>>>*Message begins*

Justicius Resk, I am pleased finally to bring you a little positive news. Attached to this message is the first entry from Probator Symeon Dymaxion-Noctis' journal that we have managed to decode. Alas, the transcript cipher continues to frustrate the best of our lexators. I continue to petition the Adeptus Mechanicus for official aid in decrypting the documents but they are unforthcoming. I shall persist. Forgive me, I make no excuses, I only seek to keep your honour apprised of all discoveries appertaining to this sorry affair, no matter how small.

* * *

In the meantime, there is some interest to be gleaned from Dymaxion-Noctis' account here regarding the state of his mind a few months before the incident. It is noteworthy that the journal appears to be addressed to a reader, as yet whom I have not been able to determine. Dymaxion-Noctis himself will not say. He remains remarkably stubborn in this regard. Since his district records were purged – almost certainly by his hand – it has been hard to pin anything down regarding his past. His family are deliberately obstructive, and will not release their archives to me. They have influence that goes beyond anything I can personally bring to bear, and the Adeptus Arbites have made it quite clear to me that they will not be involving themselves any further. If I may be so impertinent to ask, perhaps you might have more success with either the higher authorities or with the family? Your station is more exalted than mine; they may listen to you.

I think Dymaxion-Noctis is enjoying my frustration. His heart rate spiked when I told him we'd cracked a part of his journal, and although he was back to his usual, contemptuous self within minutes, I admit to a certain triumphalism in my attitude towards him afterward, as I felt we may be getting somewhere. For this small sin I ask forgiveness of both you and the Emperor, my lord. I assure you my enthusiasm did not affect my judgement.

The entry we decrypted comprises a mixture of audex, vid, pict and text (all materials appertaining to this document are appended to this missive [ref Omicron-7, eyes only]). However, Dymaxion-Noctis seems to favour writing as his key mode of expression. He has a bit of literary flair, so for ease of digestion I have taken the liberty of condensing the original into this text version, supplementing it in the one or two places it was necessary with words of my own based upon the other materials [see appended index for additional elements].

Your obedient s'vnt,
Fyedor Blovast, probator, first class

>>>vox-script ends
>>>decrypted entry begins

Deet-deet, deet-deet.

The vox-clarion makes a noise too much like sand biters for my liking. It reminds me of what was, before I left my life behind. *Deet-deet, deet-deet.* That's how it goes, just like the biters. Anticipation of the alarm colours my dreams, taking me down routes of memory I would rather not travel, back to the deserts on the high estates, and those few moments I enjoyed with my father.

I hate it, but I can't bring myself to change it.

My augmetic arm is difficult to control after sleep. It requires time to mesh with my nervous system. I have to work it through several exercises to encourage good synch rates. I rarely have time. As a result, I've smashed more vox-units with my steel fist than I care to admit. In my dreams my right hand is still flesh. When I awake, I don't remember that it's gone.

This time, I found the button and pressed it down. The vox-channel opened. Its distinctive click helps anchor me in the here and now. It reminds me of who and what I am.

'Noctis,' I said. I couldn't help but yawn. Last night had been a late one. Not work, just Shebeena, me and a bottle of amasec.

'*Probator, I am sorry for the earliness of the hour, but you asked to be informed.*'

I sat up and rubbed my face. The augmetic is good, but it's not real. The plasteel between the synflesh pads rasps on my stubble. It's always cold in the morning.

'I've fourteen alerts out with Bastion command, Borostin, which is it?'

My mouth felt terrible. There was a cup of cold caffeine next to my bed. I sipped it and winced, but I didn't put it down, and got out of bed.

'*Sorry, sir,*' said Borostin. He was good at his job, though he needed a bit of prodding. He's dead now. That was my fault. Another lead ingot of shame to carry. '*It is Yerzy Demedoi. The missing persons case.*'

'Marchenstka,' I said.

The missing persons case – such a bland phrase for so career-ruining an affair, I thought. There was a Lord Marchenstka, nasty piece of work, but I'll get to him some other time. His daughter Xuliana was an idealist, a bit like me, but more stupid. Because she was an idealist and more stupid than I was, she was missing. Kidnapped almost certainly. Probably dead. The children of rich men get taken for slates all the time, but there are worse kidnappings driven by the need to bring the mighty low. I figured it was that kind, because I couldn't find a trace of her. That was a problem. Pressure was being brought to bear. It was annoying me, though not as much as it was annoying Castellan Illois.

'Where is he?'

'*Chainward.*'

'Fine, got anything more specific?'

'*Yes. I have his exact location, as of three hours ago.*'

'I'll go check it out.'

There was a pause. '*There's an active sanctioner operation going on in the Chainward underside.*'

'Food riots?' There was a problem with supply to some of Varangantua. There's never been quite enough to eat on Alecto, but genuine shortages are getting normal. A lot of people are dying.

'Yes. Again. District-wide.'

'Was it the sanctioners that voxed Demedoi's position in?'

'No, sir,' said Borostin. *'Informant.'*

'Aren't they the most reliable?' I said sarcastically.

'If you're lucky, he'll still be there.'

'If I'm lucky,' I said. My head was unusually clear, and I thought the amasec must have been real for once. The real stuff is rare in Varangantua. My father once boasted there were probably only a few thousand bottles on the whole planet, but you can tell it's real when it doesn't give you a bad head. I lucked out there.

'Vox ahead, let them know I'm coming. Tell them it's a priority matter. Castellan Illois to seal-stamp it. I don't want any trouble, sanctioners are hotheads at the best of times.'

'I am on it, sir.'

'Borostin?'

'Sir?'

'Good work,' I said grudgingly, because it was good work and nobody ever gets enough praise.

'Thank you, sir,' and he was gone.

I went to the window and finished the caffeine. I live high up, it's the one concession I make to who I was. I don't let people come to my place. I don't want them to see how I live, perhaps because I feel guilty about it, even now, even when this domicile is nothing like what I grew up with. I had to make a choice. Do I deny everything I was, and live in the dirt, or do I buy myself a little comfort?

I considered living poor. I tried, for a while. I drank a

lot. I hung about in places where people with a probator's holo-seal don't go. I think I might have been trying to kill myself, being deliberately careless like that. It was a phase, it passed. In the end I figured, if I am going to do my job properly, like I said I would, swore I would when I walked out on a king's life, then I could live a little high. You don't need to wallow in the dirt to save people from it. Getting your hands grubby gives you a bit of perspective, and that's enough for me. So I live well.

I never said I was perfect.

My coat and trousers and shirt were dumped on the floor, each covered with dust. I shook them off, not caring about the mess. I have a servant. Let them take care of it. Like I said, I'm not perfect.

Shebeena gave me the big brown eyes before I left. I gave her a look to say *no*. She slinked across the floor and cried. The mewling beast wanted out.

'You can't go out,' I said. 'You can never go out,' I tell her, every day. 'If I let you out, you'll get stolen for sale or for food.' I rubbed her head. She forgave me, she always does. What I never tell her is that there are mutant felids living wild and free in the undercity, big as Maliwan tigers. She'd only get ideas.

I fed her. She gave me a hard stare, but seemed to be content with breakfast.

There's a lifter direct from my place to the vehicle park. There's a lot of rich people in my habclaves, a lot of private groundcars in the low levels. I was in my own in moments.

I don't know if you remember what Nearsteel is like this time of year, it's a long time since you left, but before it gets cold in winter, it's hot. The wind comes off the Westering Ocean, full of water, hits the barrens, then Varan Mountains, dumping the first snows and rains on the far side, then comes down on us with hot teeth of dust, and they bite hard. Some climactic effect makes it hot; it's weird, but it's natural. They say you can tell how cold the winter will be by how warm the wind is. It doesn't last long, but it was one of the hot days.

The wind feels like anger when it comes like that, and it heats up Nearsteel like a pot on a fire. It was the kind of day where violence was going to happen. You could taste it on the air, heavy, metallic, like blood. The ordinary men and women on this heap of a planet get kicked in the teeth all the time; on days like that they get one extra for free. Praise the Emperor.

Chainward is a subdistrict of Nearsteel, and right at the foot of the Steelmound. I took the Chainward road down from the upper slopes. Nearsteel crawls up the mountains, trying to escape the dirt. You can see the snow on the peaks from my place, on the rare clear day. The city is old there. Deep levels fill old valleys. Father had a map in his study. I used to look at it for hours. He encouraged me, one of the rare few times the old bastard had anything nice to say to me. There was a valley here. You can't see the valley, but you can see the shape of the mountains either side, buried under climbing ranks of habclave spires, like a mouth, full of steel teeth. Emperor alone knows what's down there underneath. We enforcers never venture far into it. Chainward is as deep as we go.

The biggest tooth of all is the Adeptus Mechanicus enclave of Steelmound, and it stabs the sky like it means it. It's a proper spire. The top is a blade that cuts the clouds, taller than the mountains ever were. At the side there's a voidport, only halfway up but most of the way into space, leaning out.

I often think of it as a mushroom, the kind that eats metal in the undercity. Sometimes I see it as a veesper nest, all the ships coming and going into the docks like insects. I've seen them bring big voidships down there, but it's small for a voidport, or so they say.

Normally I can see the Steelmound from my habclave. There's one spot I can stand in my domicile and see through the close-packed blocks on the slopes to the denial zone and the redway around the bottom. That morning I couldn't see anything. The wind brought a cloud of dust fine as a vladar's make-up. The kind you can always taste, no matter how good the filtration is, grit and dust and dryness. It makes you thirsty. It's arid, used up. That's what Alecto tastes like. A man I know, he's called Hon Jin, once told me that we're lucky, in Nearsteel, to be able to taste the planet at all. Most people in Varangantua don't get that close to nature, he says. But nature doesn't taste like that. I know better places than this. Alecto is mummified. Varangantua is a bloom of rot on the side.

The streets were empty. There were warnings of worse weather to come, ash storms and grit big enough to kill, with cold weather coming on the tail of the hot. There was a prohibition on travelling in all the mountain districts. The groundcar whispered down the road alone. Dust flew up behind and was snatched off by the wind, to rejoin the flowing ribbons coursing down over the mountains. The dust cut visibility down to fifty yards or so. With winter coming the nights were already getting into their stride. The morning was piss weak, and it wouldn't get much lighter. The sky was orange, the buildings were black shapes. The groundcar gave me guidance; I wasn't going to crash, but tech can't take away the sense of claustrophobia the dust brings.

The road bottomed out. I should have been able to see

the Steelmound poking the sky, but I couldn't see anything. Just a hint of a void where the Redway was, that empty circle that keeps Them separate from Us.

Maybe you don't know. Maybe they don't teach you *this*. I'll just lay it out. There isn't only one Imperium, not like we think of it. There's Terra and Mars. Each runs a part of the realms of mankind. Their relationship is complicated. We know that here, living so close to the Adeptus Mechanicus that we breathe their second-hand air, rich with the stinks of tech-sorcery. We live in the shadow of their hive.

I turned off into an access tunnel that headed under the weight of buildings crushing Alecto's rock, and into Chainward.

There's an environment seal on all the major undercity accesses in the mountain zones. It's cheaper to keep the dust out and let the people rebreathe the same air when the storms come than it is to try to filter the atmosphere. There are double gates, right across the road. There were three other groundcars waiting for entry, one private, two official. The gate will take forty at a time, that gives you an idea of how quiet it was, but the door opened, and on the other side, different story. People everywhere, and, that close to the surface, other groundcars. I had to turn my clarions on to join the main Chainward route. Others on the road get out of the way quickly enough. That makes me feel powerful, and I don't like it. The only thing that makes me feel better is reminding myself of the real power I gave up for this life, and the job I have to do. That puts the scared faces and the dangerous hurry as the traffic clears out of my way into perspective. It stops me feeling like any other spire-born swine lording it over the lessers.

But it still tastes sour.

* * *

'You can't go any further, Symeon. Not in your groundcar.'

'Why?' I said. I'd wound down my window to speak with Balthuis. I knew him a little. He was a decent enough man for a sanctioner. 'Didn't Borostin vox you?'

Balthuis didn't answer my question, but looked back over the barriers closing the road. 'Food riot. It's coming. We've got boots on the ground, going in to pull out the ringleaders before it gets out of hand, but it's going to start. We can't stop that.'

I nodded. 'Even if I didn't know, I'd be able to smell it. It's on the wind.' I could smell the dust too, even down there. It ground between my teeth. My eyes were dry with it.

'It's a hot wind blows no good,' he said.

'It's the war.'

'What? Keeping the food from hungry mouths?' Balthuis snorted. 'You've always been soft. When isn't there a war on somewhere?'

This is true, but what was happening out there beyond the system was like nothing ever before.

'This is just an excuse for insurrection,' Balthuis went on. 'They need to be punished.'

I drummed my hands on the guide wheel of the ground-car. 'This war's bigger than them all, so I heard.'

'You listen too much to rumours.'

'That's why I'm good at my job.'

Balthuis had his helmet off. That always looks wrong. In full gear, a sanctioner is faceless. He is a limb of the vladar's government, which is an extension of the authority of the lord commander of Alecto, and so ultimately each sanctioner represents the Imperium itself, in their own small way. They are the visible will of the Emperor. We probators could be anyone. We don't wear a uniform. The sanctioners look the part, with their armour, badges and the weapons: black and more black, the colour of authority, the colour of death.

With their helmets off, though, they look like they're pretending.

'You'll know that I shouldn't let you through, unless it's official.'

'It's official. Borostin told you.' I was pretty sure they'd spoken.

'I need to see the papers,' said Balthuis.

Of course he did. You'll never see a sanctioner give up the chance to lord it over a probator. I leaned across the passenger seat and pulled out a data-slate from the groundcar's storage compartment. It's a mess in there. I like to keep my vehicle clean, I paid for it after all. But the box is a mess. Food wrappers, penance scripts, all sorts gets shoved in there until it can take no more, then I empty it out and start again. Balthuis raised an eyebrow at the difference between the mess and the pristine, polished plastek of the rest of the interior.

'What can I say?' I said. 'I like a little contrast in my life.'

He shook his head. The gesture of a down-to-earth man dismissing the pretensions of the higher classes. They all hate me for what I was. They think *I'm* pretending. Balthuis took the slate. It was a department-issue, and activated in proximity to the ident-bead buried in his wrist.

'Detention warrant?' He read the name on the file. 'Yerzy Demedoi.'

'Like Borostin said.'

'Let's assume your underling didn't get me. Warrant,' he repeated.

'It's only a warrant if I need it to be,' I said. 'I need to talk to that man. He might have a lead on a case I have, but I don't want to bring Demedoi in if I don't have to.' I waved my real hand vaguely. 'Too many ripples of the wrong kind.'

'I don't care what you're doing,' said Balthuis. 'But this says you can go.' He frowned again. 'If you don't need to arrest him, why do you have the detention warrant?'

'I smelled what's coming,' I said, gesturing at the air as if I could still smell the wind as well as I could still taste the dust. He followed it with suspicious eyes. I wear a glove to cover the augmetic, but people know about it. Augmetics stir up all kinds of emotions, most bad. 'And I like to do things properly.'

'Then I'm going to have to let you in.' Balthuis frowned. 'Leave the groundcar there.' He pointed to a stretch of oily pavement two feet wide running alongside the carriageway.

'Seriously?'

'I'll watch it. You're not taking it into Deeper Chainward. All travel in and out is at our discretion.'

He gave a piercing whistle and waved at one of his men. The rumble of a heavy engine set up. Thick blue exhaust fumes pumped from an armoured vehicle.

He picked up the vox-bead dangling from his throat. 'Omnicast,' he ordered it. It chimed. 'All units, Probator Symeon Noctis inbound to operational zone. Do not inter-fere.' He dropped the bead and let it dangle again from its wire. 'My orders are to maintain this perimeter, and to permit no traffic through – beyond that, I have no interest. If you see any action, stay out of it. The men are all pumped up on stimms and their orders are to hit anything first, interrogate later.'

'Aren't those their orders all of the time?' I said. His eyes hardened. You can fault the sanctioners for a lot of things, but disloyalty isn't among them.

'One of my men will take you in,' he said slowly, 'then you're on your own. I like to do things properly too.'

Balthuis' driver was a sullen man who wouldn't give up his name. After asking twice without response I went in the back of the Bulwark and sat down. They are not the most comfortable vehicles. Huge wheels make the ride tolerably smooth, but the belly is close to the ground to stop people getting under it, and if it hits anything in the road it rings like a damn bell. If the Bulwark catches something, it screeches until it gets scraped off. There's no suspension to speak of, and little acoustic baffling. The barrier blade on the front restricts the view from the front window whether it is up or down. It's hot, noisy, and because of the nature of its usual passengers, it stinks. I couldn't think in there, so I extended my stun stick, checked the charge, then put it away again. I also pulled out my gun, made sure I had a bullet in the chamber, then placed it loosely in my armpit holster.

The Bulwark lurched to a halt.

'We're here, probator.'

'His Hand,' I said, giving the normal professional courtesy. The driver didn't look back. The scowl I gave him was lost on the back of his head. The side doors squealed open and I stepped out. Balthuis' man was already turning the vehicle around before I was clear, and I jogged out of the way.

The Bulwark backed up, finished its turn and growled off, leaving me in a single-lane tunnel. It was narrow and low, the kind they send servitor carts down. Chainward is dirt poor, and none but the arterial roads see much traffic.

The tunnel curved round. Orange lumens made a glowing spine along the ceiling. It was stiflingly hot with little air movement. Sometimes, if the population become rebellious, they'll turn off the air to places like this, until the ruckus dies down, but I'd had no notice of air cessation, though that didn't mean it wouldn't happen.

'Another damn thing I've got to take on trust,' I grumbled.

I rolled up my jacket sleeve and activated the cogitator I wear on my augmetic arm. I don't like direct visual feeds. Visor displays are worse. Both distract you. I keep my information where it belongs, where I can get at it easily, but only when I want it. A probator needs to use his eyes. Too many men are occupied with their info-feeds. They miss things. Spending all your time watching data screed is a good way to be bad at your job.

The arm unit has a built-in data-slate with a decent screen, high-fidelity crystal unit with hololithic projection capabilities. It's another thing my family paid for. They don't give this kind of tech out to people of our rank. Like my arm, and the car. Flashing wealth doesn't do me many favours, but I suppose I don't care, or I wouldn't do it. Way I see it, the money helps with the work. Nobody understands that it is all about the work with me.

I called up a cartolith to show me the way. Whistling, I set off down the tunnel.

In a few minutes I was on the inner ring way, Chainward's main via that goes right the way around the Steelmound. It's high enough for buildings several dozen storeys tall, and wide in places. The district had a heavy atmosphere. There was no one about. I saw a couple of shadows pull back from the windows of the high tenements, but that was it. Those not gathering for the confrontation with the sanctioners had hidden themselves away. The people in places like that always know what's going to happen before we do.

I was completely underground. There was a ceiling up there somewhere that was the underside of a more fortunate district. Chainward's one of those miserable places that never sees the sun. Tenements filled all of one side of the via, on the other was a bewildering maze of shacks, workshops and small manufactoria. Varangantua has a lot of industry, but most of the poor, and that's mostly everybody, can't afford what's made in the official manufactoria. If you want a spoon or a shirt or a gun and you're poor, this is the kind of place where you come.

I'd been here before, many times. Usually Chainward was a racket of activity. The air was unusually clear; that wasn't a good sign. It meant nobody had fired up their furnace or cookhouse, which meant whatever was going on down there had been brewing for at least a day. I had to be quick. Luckily, I didn't have far to go. I headed into the warren of workshops, loose metal sheeting that made up the streets banging underfoot, until I reached the edge.

This is why they call it Chainward. The Steelmound punches down through the layered undercity to the valley floor, then through the crust. Some say it goes all the way down, to where the rocks go soft and hot enough to cook you. On the nominal surface there's the Redway to divide Alecto sovereign territory from that of the Adeptus Mechanicus. It's not so clear-cut underground.

Golden chain hangs in a curtain to mark the periphery, following the red line on the surface that separates our bit of no-man's-land from their bit of no-man's-land. For the first vertical hundred yards or so, the delineation is obvious and severe. I stood close to the curtain and looked up. You can see up to the underside of the Redway, all the way. There's a clear space of two hundred yards at the top, a hundred yards either side of the curtain, but below that it begins to get messy, narrowing as the AdMech tower spreads its base, and the men and women of Chainward fill more of the space at the edge, getting closer and closer to the chains. Like the Imperium itself, I suppose. A division between the Adeptus Mechanicus and the rest of men that exists only on the surface. Past a hundred yards deep, the Chainers build their hovels and workshops right up to the edge, and on the other side, the Mechanicus have a proliferation of machinery. In places, they almost touch, only a thin curtain of shining alloy links keeping one world separate from the other. In other places there are heaps of shacks, Varangantuan vernacular, the academics laughingly call this kind of building, that finish at an abrupt chasm plunging down.

The chain itself is always pristine. It shimmers with a thin coating of oil. Though it's not the weirdest thing I've seen, it's weird enough. The border looks flimsy but it is real. Put a hand through that curtain and you'll lose it. If you go through you'll die. They can do that in the Steelmound – kill you dead, no matter who you are, and there's not a thing I, any enforcer, arbitrator, aristocrat or anyone else on this used-up husk of a world can do about it.

There was a narrow way between the backs of the workshops and the chains, little more than an alleyway. There was junk and metal scraps in heaps waiting to be reused, and hard not to fall over. I had my gun in my left hand. I shoot that way now. It doesn't feel right in my right any more. I was ready. I checked my location on a tri-d map. Cartolith's the only way to be sure of good navigation in a place like that. A steady red light shone on the map, marking the hovel-cum-ironsmith's Yerzy was hiding out in.

I took a moment. My breath was loud in my ears. I was

painfully aware of the junk at my feet. One wrong step would announce my presence to the cyborg masters of the Steelmound three miles above my head, never mind the scum I needed to grab a hundred yards away.

I heard it then, the chanting. Large groups of people, hundreds. The riot. I came to myself a little, reconsidered my position.

I cast a look down the back of the shacks piled up by the fall of flawless gold links. I was in a good place to get ambushed.

I decided to go in through the front.

I took a passage away from the chain and back out onto the main thoroughfare. It was only half-accurately portrayed by my cogitator. Things change down in Chainward all the time. Someone had straightened the road out, zoned the buildings, tidied things up. I thought it could be the work of a rising burgrave, behaving responsibly as he trod the blind path that leads from altruist to crime lord. I'd seen it happen a thousand times. Best intentions are no guardians of morals.

There was a line of sanctioners blocking the road, two ranks, forty yards across, for the way had been widened considerably there. The roads were built wide in ancient times, you can tell when you look at it carefully. Shanty towns and rickety factories spring up, crowding them like weeds before being cut back. It's the cycle of life in the lower city. At the moment, the main way looked almost impressive.

The enforcers were backing up from the line in lockstep, stamping their feet and slamming their riot shields down in time. The thunder of law enforcement boomed off metal skies.

The crowd refused to listen. They were shouting all at once, singing uncoordinated snatches of songs about injustice and oppression. They're all bad, those songs, and the singers didn't know more than half the words.

A vox-amplified voice barked from the centre of the sanctioner line.

'Return to your habs! Return to your toil! You are in violation of the Lex-Alecto. Disperse, or suffer the consequences.'

He didn't quote which articles of the law he referred to, or where it came from. There was no point. He could have been making it up on the spot. As far as the rioters believed, he probably was.

The crowd moaned and cooed. It's a strange noise, so many people together. People lose themselves in crowds. It becomes one beast, with one voice, as loud and layered as that of the sea. *Food*, it was shouting. *Hungry. Unfair.* Drums rumbled. Metal clashed on metal.

'Return to your homes!' the leader shouted. I didn't recognise his voice, and I could not see from which sanctioner it came. I probably knew him, but they were supposed to be faceless, and it worked.

I didn't have time to watch this. Yerzy's hidey-hole was still some fifty yards behind the retreating sanctioners, but they'd soon back up past it. I ran up behind them, making sure to broadcast my presence to them. They didn't turn, but they knew I was there.

'Present mauls!' their leader shouted. They parted their shield wall a little, showing their shock mauls. They thumbed them on. Lightning flickered down the line. That got the crowd's attention, and it stopped, but this was going to get bloody. It was written in the stars. I moved quietly along the street towards the ironsmith's, trying to outrun the approaching violence.

At that moment, Yerzy put his head out a first-floor window

to see what was going on. I was certain he was going to see me. For a long second he watched the protest, then, inevitably, he decided to look back. He saw me. His eyes widened; he knew I was coming for him. His head pulled back in and he vanished.

I swore, and ran. The door exploded inward to a punch from my augmetic arm. There were three women and a number of children in a small room. They screamed as I burst in. I shoved them out of the way to get to the narrow stairs behind them. As I cleared the first three steps, las-shot seared away the gloom and lit up a heat spot on the metal wall, but it was wild, and I took the chance that Yerzy was running and would not shoot again.

'Yerzy Demedoi, if you're innocent, you'll stop!' I said, then threw myself around the corner of the stairs. I didn't fire. I needed Yerzy alive.

He wasn't innocent. He knew I knew that, so he was running. Through a door thrown back so violently it jammed open I saw his heels vanishing through a window. He took quite a leap, I'll give him that – head first, arms out, over a narrow cut-through. He hit the roof on the other side, rolling agilely and springing up. He looked back. He was nimble, but breathless. No one down there has health worth a damn. I took a shot then, grazing sparks from the thick plasteel by his feet. Legshots are hard. It's why you're supposed to aim for the centre of mass on a target, but Yerzy could live without a leg. He needed his heart and lungs to talk. He fired back wildly, a las-bolt flicking on then off and scoring black carbon on the ceiling. I was more cautious going through the window than he, mindful I was a good target, but he wasn't waiting, instead scampering up a ramp to a higher roof and running.

'Stop!' I shouted.

He didn't stop.

I jumped, glad that the noise of our weapons was swallowed up in the noise of the protest. The sanctioners were on a hair trigger. They were going to charge the crowd. That's what they do, it's inevitable, but I didn't want to be the man to set them off. There's enough blood on my hands.

We were running above the crowd. The smell of them was intense, a hot, rising wind of unwashed bodies and incipient sickness. But they were energetic in taunting the line, banging their drums, shouting and singing.

Yerzy sprinted hard along the rooftops. I followed him. I made a long jump coming down on a shanty roof that nearly caved in. He bounced from roof to roof with practised ease, but I was faster. Yerzy was your standard low-city peon, stunted by years of erratic nourishment. A benefit of my job is better food than most citizens will ever see. Then there's my family connections. The bottom line is, I was a lot healthier than him. I gained on him. Nearer, nearer. He jumped, simian light, landing in a crouch on a corrugated plastek roof. It bounced as he loped to the other side. I followed him.

Being healthier means being heavier.

I landed on the roof of a shack while he was still crossing it. The plastek gave way, and we both fell into the building. We landed on metal struts and broken plastek sheets, me more awkwardly than him. He was up first. The Emperor must have spared me a little blessing, for Yerzy had lost his gun. I still had mine. I pointed it at him, freezing him on the brink of the building.

'Where is she, Yerzy? Where's the Marchenstka girl?'

'I don't know what you're talking about!' he said. His voice was ruined by years of bad air. His eyes slipped sideways down to the street, judging the leap. We were twenty feet up. That's a long way to jump.

'Don't even think about it,' I said. 'It'd be better if you came with me now.'

'We both know that's not true,' he said. He jumped. I fired. I missed him again. I've never been a great shot, with my left hand I'm worse than I was before. I needed more time on the range. There was a heavy length of rail pinning my leg down, but it wasn't hard for my augmetic to lift. The limb is strong, but the muscles and bone it attaches to are those of a mortal man, and I felt hot, tearing pain as the machinery kicked in.

I was on my feet in time to see Yerzy blundering up from a tangle of limbs. He pushed his way through people, stirring up an angry current in the ebb and flow of the crowd.

'Stop!' I shouted. I didn't dare fire again. Too many people. Too many sanctioners waiting for an excuse.

Cursing, I jumped down after him. I had a worse landing, hitting hard ground rather than soft bodies. A spike of pain shot up my shin into my knee. I ignored it, hobbling on and cursing. My arm hurt, my knee hurt.

'Yerzy, get back here!' I pushed my way through a living forest of limbs and bodies. It was hot in the crowd, and the smell was overpowering. Faces flashed by me in a variety of shocked and outraged expressions. Yerzy's blundering progress left a channel of displaced bodies, and once or twice I caught sight of him ahead, looking back. Now it was his time to move quickly. He was smaller, wiser to the ways of crowds like this, and his Throne-damned knee wasn't on fire like mine.

I could have fired my gun, I could have proclaimed who

and what I was. I'd like to think you're smart enough to see how damn stupid that would have been.

Yerzy was wise to his advantages over me, and was cutting back down through the protest, directly away from me and putting more distance between us with every moment. He was trying to get far enough ahead that I couldn't see where he was going, then he'd be off into the buildings away from the Steelmound and I'd never find him again.

A horn blared. The enforcers roared. The time had come, they were charging the crowd. I could hear the buzz and crack of shock mauls. The crowd bunched up. The movement within became chaotic. Singing and shouts turned to screams.

'Terra condemn us all,' I whispered. I keyed a rune on my cogitator, sending a cocktail of stimm and painkiller into my bloodstream. The pain from my injuries immediately diminished. I was still aware of it, but it was reduced to a warm, pleasant glow.

Then I raised my gun and fired.

'Down, down, down! Probator business!'

There were screams then. People were too panicked by the approaching sanctioners to react violently to me, scattering instead. They tripped up and fell outward, like an opening flower. I got a clear look at Yerzy, some forty feet away, and went after him. My knee ground, but painlessly. The crowd's opening made it easier for him too, and he shoved his way out. The sanctioners were coming deeper into the crowd, standard riot-breaking tactics. They don't take the brightest as enforcer recruits, and they're nothing if not predictable. A wedge of men, driving into the group, lashing out on all sides as they came. The crowd buckled. They call these riots, but mostly they're not, not until we get involved. Most of the people were fleeing, bashing into me. But others were turning back to fight, going against combat-conditioned sanctioners in full armour kit with nothing more than lengths of pipe and bred-in grievance.

I couldn't catch up to Yerzy, but I could trap him. I angled away from the Steelmound and the chain barrier, pushing him towards the workshop shanty around the exclusion zone. He was looking over his shoulder, but he saw me, and the approaching phalanx of enforcers. The crowd was scattering, movement was easier, so I began to run again, Yerzy made to go into the tenements where people were fleeing, but I shook my head, moving quicker to push him back inward. Seeing the sanctioners about to catch him, he forced his way past the running people and back into the ring of workshops around the Steelmound's roots.

I followed before my less-refined colleagues could catch up.

I was in a big shed, high ceiling, lots of rusty chains hanging down and rows of lathes occupying the floor. Yerzy was in there somewhere, in that place they made Emperor-knew-what for Emperor-knew-who.

I went slow now. My heart was hammering from the stimms and my leg was dangerously hot, but everything was crystal clear and sharp. I was going to suffer for it the day after, but right then, the world was a vibrant place, and every danger a challenge.

Gunfire started from across the street, sounding small and ridiculous at that distance. The crowd's screams were thin as the wails of the seabirds in the ocean districts. Sanctioners bellowed threats. They were kicking in the doors, harsh crashes that came closer, but it was still quiet enough for me to hear Yerzy's blundering progress. I followed him. His poorer health was telling, and he was slowing. The irony was, his masters probably cared about him more than the supposedly legitimate owners of this district did about the inhabitants. But his bosses didn't care enough. It's how I always get these people, through the soft, unprotected underbelly of the abused and dispossessed. I almost felt sorry for him.

Yerzy was panting loudly. It echoed around the machine shop.

'I can hear you, Yerzy! You sound like a broken engine!' I shouted. 'Just stop, man, let's talk.'

'They'll kill me! They'll kill my family!' he shouted back.

I swivelled to where his voice came from, and walked stealthily. My knee was stiff, swelling making my gait unsure, throbbing with heat like a fusion reactor, but I kept my weapon up. I panned the gun around, holding it in both hands, covering the corners, the girders overhead, the bases of benches, anywhere he might be hiding. I got close, and he made a break for it. They always do.

He ran rat-fast down an aisle between two rows of workbenches towards a door leading out to the chain guard. I followed him, a living finger resting on the trigger. I took my time, waiting for a clear shot. There was a line of pallets of rusty scrap in between him and the door. He had to climb it. This time when I fired, I hit him.

He gave a cry. A dark stain bloomed on his trouser leg. He pitched forward off a pallet and crashed down. Little bastard had a lot of fight in him, because he got up, limping on his wounded leg towards the door. I went after him, hardly more graceful. I could barely bend my knee, and had to walk around the scrap.

He was failing fast. He had got out of the door, but couldn't manage more than that and was crawling when I found him again. Death was walking patiently behind him, and I'm not talking metaphorically about myself. I must have nicked an artery in his leg, because he was pissing blood, leaving a wide smear on the metal.

The chains were twenty feet away from the back of the manufactory. On the other side the gap between Alecto and forge world sovereign territory opened up. There was a darkness there that suggested a deep shaft, and a constant draught blowing up from somewhere that made the chains sway and chink for a hundred yards in both directions. I could hear machinery murmuring to itself. Lights shone in the thickets of pipes on the Martian side.

I raised my gun, taking aim at his back. I didn't need to. I'd already killed him.

'Unburden yourself, Yerzy Demedoi. Tell me where the Marchenstka girl is.'

'You're no priest,' he gasped, doggedly clawing his way over the plated metal ground to the chains.

'The Emperor will punish you if you die with evil in your heart.'

'Screw the Emperor!' he snarled. He was by the chains. The pit yawned. He dragged himself to the very edge, and rolled on his back to look me in the eye. He was breathing fast and shallow, in that way the dying do. 'The Emperor's done nothing for me, not ever. He condemned me and all my kind to live in this hole in the ground. So sincerely, He can go fuck Himself with His own Throne-damned holy golden sword.'

'I can save you,' I said. 'You don't have to die. Get that hole patched up in your leg. You help me, there'll be a reward.'

He laughed. 'Yeah, a hail of bullets or a sinner's pyre. The lords and ladies are not the forgiving types.'

I stood over him. 'I won't shoot you.'

'I know,' he said.

'I'll help your family.'

He grinned, defeated. 'I half believe that. I've heard you're a good man, Noctis. More fool you, I say. What use has Varangantua for good men?'

'You don't have to die,' I said. I holstered my gun to show I meant it.

He smiled. 'You know what we say down here? We're all born dead.'

I could see it coming. I lunged for his leg, but he hauled himself over the lip of the drop with arms wiry with a lifetime of relentless work, and fell soundlessly into the dark.

There was a loud crack, the kind generated by a large las discharge, and a flash. I put my head by the chains, but knew not to put it through. I saw nothing beyond the swaying of the links.

I sighed. The stimms and anaesthetic were wearing off. My knee and side were beginning to hurt. I limped back towards the machine shop. There was noise and danger on the far side of that building, but nowhere else to go.

Three sanctioners burst out of the door. They saw the blood, they saw me.

'Stop, in the name of the Lex-Alecto!'

'I'm stopped,' I said. I held up my hands. 'You can lower your weapons. I am Pro–'

One of them had a webber and a vicious need to use it. He sprayed me with a cloud of constricting filaments that squeezed the air out of my lungs and the ability to talk with it. One of the others held up his maul to the side of my head, turned down the charge, then tapped me on the temple.

I hate those things. Like being punched by an ogryn. Everything went away for a while.

I was still peeling bits of web off my coat when the Bulwark door slid back.

'You look like shit,' said Balthuis. He was grinning. He's a bag of asses, that man, but I kind of like him.

'My head hurts, my knee's shot and I tore all the muscles down my side.'

'Fancy augmetics do you no favours,' Balthuis said.

I got up off the bench. In truth, a lot more than head, knee and side hurt. All of it did, apart from my metal arm, and because of that it felt more alien than usual.

'Try saying that when you lose an arm,' I said. I limped out.

'My men will be disciplined,' he said.

'Yeah, before or after you buy them a drink?'

He rested his hand on my shoulder. I winced.

'Did you get your man?'

'No,' I said. 'Let's say he found his own way out of Varangantua's miseries.'

'Too bad,' he said. I think he meant it.

'Too bad,' I said, and limped back across the road to my groundcar. I had a felid to feed. Nothing much else seemed important right then.

'See you around, Symeon Noctis!' Balthuis shouted.

I ignored him, and let the autodrive take me home.

I'm writing this later that same day. I'm still messed up. My knee will take a week to fix, at least. The winds are dropping. The rains will follow, then the snow; it's only a few days now. Winter's herald has blown his trumpet, as the half-slate seers say down on Tinker's Row. I still haven't found the

Marchenstka girl. Demedoi was my best lead, and I lost it. This is going to be problematic.

I don't know if you'll ever read these words. I don't know if I can find you. And if I do, what then? You'll be changed. Wherever they sent you, Alecto will just be one world to you, Varangantua one city among millions of other grimy shitholes. The best I can hope for is that you'll read these accounts, and you'll get to know me, a little, as a man. I hope you don't condemn me for what I am.

I don't know what kind of man I am. Perhaps I'll find out too.

Maybe Yerzy was right. Maybe I am good a man, and maybe that does make me a fool. His words trouble me now.

What use does Varangantua have for good men?

Decrypted journal entry ends>>>>>>

YOUR
NEXT READ

BLOODLINES
by Chris Wraight

An investigation into a missing member of a wealthy family leads Probator Agusto Zidarov into a web of lies and danger amidst the criminal cartels of Varangantua. As the net closes in, Zidarov falls further into darkness from which he may never return…

WARHAMMER™
HORROR

The Reaper's Gift

Ray Cluley

Rutger ran through the wet cornfield, staggering between withered stalks, slipping in mud, one arm hooked around his stomach to slow the blood. A weak rain hung in the air like mist. The sky was thick with cloud and all colour had seeped away to something purple-tinged, like a contusion. Rutger held up a hand to protect his face from the crops, barely able to see where he was going in the descending darkness.

He glanced behind, as he'd done countless times over miles he barely remembered, but all he saw was stalks of corn closing behind him in broken rows. Some were bent out of shape, bloodied by his passing; others drooped with the weight of their own rot. Trampled stalks pressed beneath his boots were slow to rise again, and the prints he'd left in the mud were filling with small puddles. He would be easy to track, even in this dying light.

A furrowed row, mud-thick and slick with rain, sent him stumbling and he added a handprint to those of his boots, pushing up from the ground to continue fleeing. He turned with the direction of the crops and followed them for a few moments of easier progress, then turned again for the safety of their cover.

Amongst the corn were tangled low growths of bloodweed. Some of it burst underfoot as he ran, souring the soil with its dark, poisonous sap. Where it was thickest it snatched at his ankles and threatened to trip him. It was said that upon land where battles had been fierce the bloodweed grew, and there was nowhere in Shyish that had not known battle. It thrived where blood had been spilt in vast quantities, keeping the killing fields red and spreading to choke whatever else might grow. It was desperately difficult to farm such land, but evidently there were those who tried. Rutger cursed them for not ploughing deep enough before planting, for not pulling the weed properly, and he turned to find a clearer route through the rows of the cornfield.

Crows burst into sudden flight around him in a flurry of feathers that swallowed him with their darkness. He dropped into a crouch, one arm overhead to fend off the thunder of their wings. Then they were gone, lost to the early evening sky as quickly as they had erupted into being. He heard their cries and for a moment he was back on the battlefield with the screams and shrieks of the dying. With his eyes clenched shut he saw soldiers fall, carved to bloody pieces. Saw them trampled by the hooves of two-legged beasts that growled and howled as they rushed towards their next enemy, each one hefting vicious blades or wickedly tipped spears. One of them swung at him but he found his feet and ran and–

He was back in the cornfield, fleeing from a battle left far behind. The sky deepened with cloud and seemed to press upon him, slowing him, trying to claim him for its own.

'With Sigmar's strength,' Rutger began, but he was panting and could go no further with the prayer. 'With Sigmar's strength,' he tried again, but what god would listen to him anyway? Sigmar's strength was for those who had their own, and Rutger's had all but left him. He risked another look at his stomach but in the gloom saw only where his wet wound gaped and bled. He held it closed again, his sodden sleeve a makeshift bandage, and kept running, stumbling, gasping partial prayers to a god he'd left behind with the dying.

'With Sigmar's strength… I wield,' he said. 'Forging forward, never yield…'

The words came at last, a litany of habit, but he dismissed all but two of them as he ran, reciting, 'Forging forward… Forging forward…' A heartbeat rhythm to keep his legs moving, setting a pace that kept him 'forging forward… Forging forward…'

The Freeguild army was a fierce force of men and women, tough and skilled and keen to fight, but it was difficult to remain disciplined in the face of Chaos. And Rutger had seen that face up close. Seen the matted fur of its blood-drenched muzzle and smelt the foetid stink of its breath as it roared its wrath and hunger. Beasts that walked as men, horned like goats but muscled like bulls or warhorses. Armed with deadly spears and serrated blades of steel and bone, they cut through ranks of soldiers in a ferocious frenzy. Driven by bloodlust, the beasts had hacked and torn, roaring their war cries as if outraged by man's very existence. Rutger had seen friends fall and scatter and he'd fled, determined to live while others died.

He ducked into and through another line of crops, swatting a path clear and grabbing at things to keep himself upright. The strength in his legs was fading with the light. His breathing came hard and ragged. Blood oozed from his wound despite his attempts to staunch its flow, taking his warmth with it. But still he ran, driven by desperation and fear.

A sudden figure loomed out of the dark, tall and long-limbed. With a startled cry, Rutger tried to halt but fell with the abrupt action, throwing himself backwards as best he could to get away from the weapon he saw descending upon him. He brought his arms up, yelling with the pain it pulled from his open wound, only to find he shielded himself from nothing; the weapon hung suspended above him, its long curving blade refusing to fall.

Rutger cowered from a man o' straw. Tattered clothing, lumpy with old stuffing, sagged and bulged around the ropes that held it staked. Across its body, fixed in place, a scythe rusted in the rain, and above that leered a sackcloth face, slashed open in a split grin black with mould. Rutger tried to laugh but made only a strangled sound like a sob as he rolled over in his struggle to stand.

A man o' straw, slumped in a neglected field of corn. That was all. Rutger noted how its insides spilled from a seam around the waist and looked again at his own injury. He held out no hope for help, not around here, but there would be shelter, he thought. An old farmhouse, perhaps a barn. He would rest in whatever ruin he could find.

And, yes! There! Praise Sigmar!

The land sloped and he followed it down, stumbling more than running now towards the leaning shape of an old building little more than a silhouette in the fading light. He almost fell again, this time with relief, as if he could rest right here in sight of it; he was so exhausted. But he forced himself onward, gasping and bleeding and–

'Forging forward...'

* * *

Maudeline cut the last of the stunted vegetables into small, thin pieces – as if that would convince anyone there was enough – and carried them on the chopping board to where a pot heated slowly over the room's fire.

'Harren, Leese, mind out of my way.'

The children were sitting close to the fire, playing a quiet game of straw-draw on the low protruding stone of the hearth. They were too old for such games, but they went through the motions of selecting straws from the other's hand and nodding or tutting at each result. It was a game their father had taught them; perhaps they took some comfort from that. She nudged her way past and with her knife swept the vegetables into the stew. The pieces sank all too quickly. She would need to thicken it up or they'd merely be drinking their dinner tonight.

'Where's your brother?'

Harren said nothing, too focused on his turn of the game, but Leese glanced up and said, 'Chores.'

'Still?'

The girl shrugged.

Maudeline took the board and knife back to where she'd been preparing dinner. She considered the small sack of flour on the counter. Supplies were scarce. She'd have to try one of the neighbouring farms soon, but each time meant travelling further afield. Not that anyone had anything they were willing to spare.

'You cheated!'

'Did not!'

'Quiet, you two.'

'But he cheated, Ma. He took more than he should.'

'And what have I told you about men?' She had a scowl for her daughter.

'That they can't be trusted.' Leese borrowed some of her mother's scowl for her brother.

'I didn't *cheat*!'

'Let me see, then. Open your hand.'

Maudeline closed her eyes against the squabbling and wished again that their father was here. She wished it several times a day, and prayed for it nightly, but if Sigmar heard he did not seem to care. An outlier's life was a tough one, she knew, but it was all the more difficult on your own.

'Let me *see*!'

'No!'

Maudeline opened her eyes to see Harren throw his handful of straw into the fire and move away, retreating to where he'd rolled a fleece into a seat. He was done playing.

Leese leaned close to the flames to check the burning straws.

'Leese, get back. Sit down. Harren, wipe some bowls clean for dinner.'

Sometimes Maudeline wished she was the one away at war. How long before she lost Harren to a similar cause? Leese? Even little Poll liked to play soldiers, and he was growing up faster with every day that passed. Of course they'd rather wield swords than scythes; it was far easier to spill blood than till soil. And besides, you had to fight for the land before you could farm it, and there was far more glory to be had facing enemy forces than in defending lines of seed against hungry crows. Nobody sang of a farmer's toil, or told tales of their back-breaking labour.

A leather skin of wine hung from the kitchen shelf. She was saving it for her husband, but the amount she saved for him grew less each week. If he didn't come home to them soon, there'd be nothing but gritty well-water to drink.

Maudeline retrieved her shawl from a chair by the fire and wrapped it around herself, tucking her hair into its warmth. 'Keep stirring that pot, one of you.'

'Where are you going?'

Oh, Leese, where can I go?

'To remind Poll that it's dark, and dinner's near ready.'

She took the lantern pole from beside the door. They'd long ago run out of oil for the lantern, but she'd melted a candle stub behind the shelter of the glass. She lit this with a taper from the fire.

'Remember to–'

'Bar the door, and answer no stranger,' said Leese. 'We know, Ma.'

'Good.'

There wasn't wind enough to wrench the door from her but it was strong enough to lash her with rain while still inside. What had been little more than a mist hanging in the air a few hours ago was now falling in earnest. To think, she'd prayed for this not so long ago. Now, with the corn rotting in the fields and their gathered grain spoiling, she wished for just one day of sun hot enough to dry their crops.

She pulled the shawl tighter around her face and stepped into the dark, waiting under the porch eaves until she heard the door behind her barred. Only then did she head out into the rain, using the lantern pole as support across the muddy yard.

'Where are you?' she muttered, looking for some sign of her son. The feeble candlelight from her lantern cast a pallid glow across the yard, showing her just how desolate their home had become. A water pump, rusting and forlorn, leaned over a stone trough that collected shadows with the rain. From the roof behind her came the croak and creak of the ancient weathervane as it turned in the wind. It had been a gift, pewter beaten into the shape of twin comets by her husband, as if Sigmar would watch over them.

'He likes the spirit of outliers and frontier families,' he'd told her, and they had shunned the safety of a city's rule in favour of whatever freedom could be taken from the land.

'Where are you?' she asked again, thinking not only of her son but of his father, too. Wishing he'd come back to her so she could love him and hate him and figure out which was most true.

The beast's teeth were thick with gore, its breath a reek of flesh and death as it roared its hate at Rutger. It swung its weapon up in a vicious slash, sweeping from the ground and across, but Rutger launched himself back from the blade. Cleaver-like but curved, and already slick with blood, it cut the air where he'd been standing.

He lunged into the space of the weapon's wake and managed to plunge his own blade into the creature's hide. He drove it in with both hands, but the beast turned with the momentum of its swing and barged him aside with a muscled shoulder. Rutger fell, pulling his sword free and seeing the wound he'd inflicted would not be enough.

Scrambling back, kicking at the ground, he retreated from the beastman looming over him, but when it raised its weapon he ceased his retreat and threw himself upward, sword held before him with all the force of himself behind the strike. He buried the blade deep into the beast's stomach and yanked upwards with a roar of his own. A wet heat splashed his legs and rubbery lengths unspooled from the creature's opened belly. Rutger shoved the beastman back, retrieving his sword from its body as it fell.

He turned for his next enemy and found one more ready than he'd expected, a serrated blade already slashing at him. It drew across his torso and left a hot line of pain, opening the flesh of his abdomen.

He staggered back as much in surprise as from the blow itself and–

He spasmed awake with a cry, twisting from his sleep and flooding himself with pain. He clutched at the rags he'd tied around himself as a crude bandage and felt them soaked through. With a groan, he eased himself into a sitting position and set about unwinding the cloth.

The wooden floor beneath him was damp, the boards warped beneath a carpet of mildewed straw. Rain came in through a hole in the roof and the wind whistled through the gaps in the plank walls. He had only the barest memory of collapsing inside. A barn, maybe a stable, he couldn't see or remember enough to know, but it was better shelter than anything he'd had for some time. He was cold, and uncomfortable, but he was alive. For now.

He was alarmed by the continued oozing of his wound, but his insides remained insides. There was a foul smell to it all, though. Underneath the blood, some sour stench that did not bode well. He needed a healer, and soon. Hot water, salve, clean bandages.

A creak in the dark, and his wound was forgotten. A floorboard groaning under the weight of someone or something else in the gloom. Rutger grabbed for his sword, forgetting the sheath was empty, then pushed at the floor to slide further back into the shadows of the corner where he'd slept. He looked for something to serve as a weapon but found only panic when he saw he was surrounded, figures looming out from the dark. No armour, no weapons, but they floated a few feet from the floor, peering down with vacant eyes and slack mouths. Rutger cowered from them with another cry like the one he'd woken with, then saw them for what they really were.

More scarecrows, stuffed and sagging, hanging from tool-hooks on the wooden walls.

In front of him, a figure emerged from behind the slumped stump of a hay bale, moving in a low, slow prowl. This was no scarecrow, though.

'I have bad dreams too, sometimes.'

It was a child. He remained a short distance away, close to the cover of his hay pile and its shadows, squatting as if he might run or lunge. Rutger couldn't see much of him yet, but he could tell the boy was better armed than he was; the lad held a pitchfork across his knees.

'You're in our barn.'

'I am.'

The boy nodded, satisfied by the confirmation. 'Are you hurt?'

'No.'

'You look hurt.'

Rutger sat a little straighter, trying not to wince at how it pulled his stomach. 'Just resting. Then I'll be on my way.'

'You shouldn't be here.'

'No.'

The boy took a step closer and looked him over carefully. 'You *are* hurt. You're bleeding.'

'It's nothing.'

'Will you die?'

A twinge in his wound made Rutger tight-lipped with pain, though his tight breath and sharp wince provided some sort of answer, it seemed; the boy nodded.

'Ma says we all die, but not everyone really lives.'

'She sounds very wise.'

'Are *you* scared of dying?'

A beastman lunged at Rutger, its face rushing to his with a ferocious bellow. He flinched from a bite that didn't come because he was in a barn and there were no beasts here. Just this boy, waiting for an answer. *I'm terrified*, Rutger wanted to say. *I've seen what's out there, and how it hungers for us. I've looked into the blood-drenched face of Chaos and seen it grin.*

Whatever expression accompanied Rutger's thoughts, it made the boy wary. He raised the pitchfork as if to plunge the tines into Rutger's chest.

'Those frighten me, that's a certainty,' Rutger said, nodding at the closest man o' straw. It wore torn trousers much like his own, and straw spilled from holes like open wounds. A drab tunic did a better job of keeping it in, but it sprouted from the stuffed head like hair, a topknot thatch where the sack had been tied. Thick woollen crosses had been sewn for eyes, and a dye-smeared handprint, upside down, gave it a drooling mouth. The whole body drooped like a hanged man. There was even something of a noose where a knot of rope tied the head to the body.

'Reaper's gifts,' the boy said. 'We made them for the other farms but nobody needs them now.'

'Reaper's gifts?'

'To keep the Reaperman away.'

'I'm sure they'd scare anything anyway.'

'Not the Reaperman. He's a man o' straw, too.'

The boy had lowered his weapon, such as it was. Even driven by the strength of a child it would hurt plenty, so Rutger was relieved.

When the boy said, 'If you try to take it I'll have to use it,' he realised he'd been staring. The boy feigned a jab. Rutger raised his hand as if to ward off the blow, and as an apology. He saw the boy notice the blood and lowered his hand to press at his improvised bandages.

'Who's the Reaperman?' he asked.

'You don't know the Reaperman? Everybody around here knows the Reaperman.'

'I'm not from around here.'

'Aren't you a farmer?'

'No. I'm a soldier.'

'My father's a farmer and he's a soldier.'

Rutger straightened. 'Is he here?'

'He's away, fighting. Ma said he's better at farming, but he went anyway.'

'How long ago?'

The boy shrugged, but it didn't matter. Rutger could tell from the look of the place that the boy's father had been gone a while.

'Can I see?' the boy asked. He pointed at Rutger's stomach.

'No.'

'I can help you.'

'It's too dark.'

The boy put down his weapon and reached behind the drooping hay bale where he'd been hiding. He retrieved a lantern and opened the shutter to reveal the stump of a candle, burning. The inside of the barn was bathed in a weak and flickering light. It struck the hanging strawmen so they seemed to move out of their own shadows.

'Show me,' the boy said as he approached, 'and I'll tell you about the Reaperman.'

It seemed a fair trade.

* * *

Maudeline clutched her shawl tight around her face and peered out into the drizzle, lantern held before her on its staff. She went to the chicken coop where Poll was meant to have gathered whatever eggs their scrawny bird might have managed to squeeze out. If their circumstances didn't change soon, she would have to put it in the pot for dinner, though she feared that once plucked, all she'd have to show for it would be the poor bird's bones.

It was scratching at the dirt, so Poll had tossed it something to eat at least. But where was he? After the chicken he was supposed to–

A noise in the dark snatched the rest of her thought away. A gruff breath, she'd thought, like the snort of a horse. And maybe the quick creak of wood as if it pulled against some nearby hitching post. But the farm hadn't known a horse since… well, a long time. And there was no hitching post. Only the boards of the coop, and the line of fencing around it.

The chicken *bhuk-awwed!* in alarm and flustered a panicked path, this way and that.

Maudeline did not call out. Anyone out here at this time would not mean them well, and it would be senseless to alert them that she had heard something of their movements. If it were an animal, then she didn't want it alerted either; their larder desperately needed restocking. She drew the slim blade she always carried in the front of her apron. It was the sharpest and most prized of her kitchen wares, good for the toughest of meat. It would do.

She approached the far side of the coop, keeping distance enough between her and the small pen that anyone hiding there couldn't lunge at her from its cover, but before she could see there was a quick galloping sound in the mud and then a rustle of corn. Shortly after that, from across the yard, came a short, sharp cry. A quick shriek she recognised.

'Poll!'

Maudeline ran, dropping the lantern in her haste as she hurried towards the barn.

Behind her, a puddle found its way into the lantern glass and doused the candle's forgotten flame.

Rutger made shadow shapes on the wall, enjoying the warmth of the candlelight on his hands and pleased with how each shape he made delighted the child. His father had taught him several by the glow of the forge; rabbits, horses, tavern-tale monsters. Rutger repeated as many as he could remember. The dragon had been poor – using both hands had brought some pain – but the boy had shrieked with a delight that surprised and pleased him.

He was making crows from shadows when a woman burst into the barn. Her abrupt entrance forced Rutger into a hasty retreat, despite the pain that came with it. The woman's eyes were wide, and wet hair clung to her face, but Rutger focused most on the knife she held. It looked sharp.

The woman pointed her weapon with one hand while the other beckoned to her boy. 'Come on now, Poll.'

'Ma, this is Rutger, he's–'

'To me, now, come on. Your supper is ready.'

'He's a soldier like father but not a farmer, and–'

'Poll!'

The boy flinched but was only quiet for a moment. 'He can make shapes out of shadows with his hands! Show her the dragon.'

'You should go to your mother, boy.'

The boy finally did as he was told, and the woman pulled him to stand behind her. 'Pick up your lantern.'

The shifting light sent the shadows dancing up the walls and for a moment Rutger felt himself swallowed by the dark, taken by scarecrows.

'He's hurt, Ma.'

It gave her pause, though she'd surely seen as much for herself already. 'Looks bad,' she said.

'Not many with worse get to talk about it,' Rutger admitted.

'You alone?'

'Yes.'

She stared at him. Eventually she said, 'You can come inside. There's not much food to share, but we will.'

'Praise Sigmar for you.'

'Praise my boy, he's the one found you.' She helped Rutger to stand after watching him struggle for a moment. Blood that had pooled in his lap poured to the floorboards with the sound of a drink spilled. Rutger groaned.

'I'll stitch that up before you eat,' the woman said. 'No sense feeding you just to see it all fall out again after. Come on.' She put an arm around him, and he tried to do the same to her as she led him outside, Poll bearing the light before them.

'Harren, serve supper for your brother and sister,' Maudeline said, carrying Rutger inside and to the table. 'Keep mine and our guest's in the pot for now.' It was all she gave them as an introduction, though Poll told them, 'He was in the barn. He's a soldier.'

'Sit down,' Maudeline told Rutger, easing him into a chair she'd turned away from the table.

'He's hurt.'

'Yes, Leese, he's hurt. Now eat your supper.'

Maudeline knelt beside Rutger, using her body to block any view the children might get of his wound as she peeled away his shirt. The smell beneath was so foul that she was forced to turn her head as she pulled the last of his makeshift bandages away. They stuck to his flesh, crusted to the split in his skin, and he hissed as they came free. Maudeline dropped the sodden rags into a bowl already dark with blood.

'I'll need to clean it first. You can hold it, but I'll need to get in under your hands with a hot cloth before I stitch you back together.'

Rutger clenched his teeth. His breathing came hard and fast through his nose.

'What did this?' she asked him.

The memory was instant and jarring, a beast with a savage cry of promised pain as it attacked. Rutger flinched.

'Was it a sword? An axe?'

'Something like the two together,' Rutger said. 'But as long as a spear.'

The woman – Maudeline – leaned closer, her nose wrinkled against the stench coming from his wound. 'Well, it's cut you wide open, but I don't know how much damage has been done inside. I can't see.'

She looked up at him. She'd wiped sweat from her brow and a line of his blood was smeared across her forehead. She had a stern face, tough looking, like weathered iron. He'd known women like her in the army. Her youth had worn away with hard work and children, who were likely much the same thing, but whatever hardships she'd endured only made her features more striking.

'Just stitch it closed for now,' Rutger said.

'For now,' she said. They both knew that *for now* was probably as long as he was likely to get. But she cleaned the wound as best she could. It was ragged in places, flesh torn where it hadn't been cut. She pointed it out to Rutger who grunted, remembering the wicked points of the weapon's serrated edge.

'Tricky to stitch,' she said.

'Then I'll have an interesting scar.'

His skin, pale as fish belly, was numb to each press of her needle when it came, but the pull of coarse thread through him was like a rough fire. He thought of the scarecrows hanging in the barn, splitting their stitches in the dark.

'Your son was telling me about the Reaperman,' Rutger said, keen to distract himself from what she was doing.

Maudeline looked at Poll, who was rushing his supper. 'Before or after your chores?'

'After,' he said between spoonfuls, his full attention on his meal.

'He mentioned a reaper's gift.'

'Reaping gift,' she said.

Rutger's expression encouraged her to explain.

'Around here, harvest can be hard. Not much grows without a lot of work. Did you come down through the crops? You must have. Did you see the weeds?'

Rutger grunted. 'We call it bloodweed where I'm from.'

'I've heard that. It's corpse-wort here. Crops rot, my husband calls it. Because it steals the goodness from the soil and strangles what we try to grow. Makes farming tough.'

Rutger believed it. The life he'd known before soldiering was as a farrier's son, and that had been hard work, the smithing part especially, but given the right amount of heat, metal could be shaped and manipulated far more easily than nature. Their lives out here would be constant hard work.

Rutger hissed and shifted in his chair as Maudeline pulled the thread tight to knot it. She withdrew her small blade from the front pocket of her apron and cut away the excess.

'There were a dozen or so families out here not that long ago,' she said, 'each with their own reasons for living as outliers. When one of us had a bad harvest, the rest contributed so as no one would starve or suffer for the next planting. Called it a reaping gift. If we couldn't contribute crops, some other gift was given to show they had the charity of our thoughts, if little else.'

'Like a man o' straw.'

'If you were lucky you'd get something useful, yes. Crows can be as much a problem as crops rot out here. But it could as likely be a ragdoll or wooden toy.'

'Or stitches, and a bowl of hot food.'

She nodded. 'Here, hold this.' She pressed a folded piece of clean cloth to the long, jagged crescent of his black-stitched wound.

'And the Reaperman?' Rutger asked.

'The Reaperman comes for you if you don't give a reaping gift,' Poll said without looking up from his soup. He was scraping his spoon against the bottom of the bowl as if he might work some of the wood into his meal. 'He's like a giant man o' straw so he can't die and sometimes he has a stuffed sack for a head and sometimes a huge gord–'

'And sometimes he has a rusty scythe,' Harren added, warming to their guest, 'like the one in our field. Or sometimes he has two bloody sickles for hands and he comes for you if you don't give what you could to those who needed it.'

'Or if you're not grateful when someone else gives you something,' said the girl, Leese. She gave him a hard stare.

'Well, I'm grateful,' he said.

'Leese, get me something I can use for a fresh bandage.' Maudeline pointed at a trunk pushed against the wall. The girl left the table to do as she was told. Maudeline helped Rutger turn around to face the bowl Poll had ladled full for him.

Rutger spooned the broth so eagerly that most spilled down his chin, much to Poll's delighted astonishment. It tasted more like water that vegetables had once been washed in, but he found a few tiny morsels worth chewing and it was hot, as promised. The heat of it was perhaps the most delicious part.

'This is good,' he said.

'It's not, but you're welcome to it.' Maudeline sat with an empty bowl. She leaned over it to say quietly, 'To hear the Reaperman is to hear death calling for you.' She glanced at where Rutger held the cloth against himself. 'You'll likely hear him soon.'

Rutger paused in his eating. The children were solemn. If the woman was trying to joke with him, she needed practice.

'Not a ghostly scream coming at you out of the dark,' Maudeline explained, 'not some banshee's shriek or wailing cry of woe. Just the whispered doom of his scythe, like a swathe of cut corn, or the wind whistling through the crops. And then he's there to take all you have left.' She eased back into her chair. 'Leese, what are you doing? Just bring me one of the shirts.'

Leese had a pile of clothes beside her at the trunk. She pulled a shirt from them.

'Put the rest back as neat as you found them.'

'Don't ruin a good shirt on my account,' Rutger said.

Maudeline waved the comment away.

'He was a healer, once,' she said. 'The Reaperman. Living

with his wife where the Harden farm is now. They had a strong ox to pull their plough and come the harvest they always had an abundance of crops which they'd share amongst the other farms. What they lacked was children, and children are what we outliers have for farmhands, but they kept trying and eventually they managed one. Bligh, they called him. He wasn't a strong worker, but he was keen and helped as much as he could. Certainly more than these three.'

The children protested and she smiled, hushing them. To Rutger she admitted, 'They make my life easier as much as they make it difficult. Do you have any?'

'No.'

She nodded once at that, as if the answer satisfied her in some way.

'Anyway, Bligh died,' she said.

'How?'

'He fell under the plough,' Maudeline said. 'Dragged a full length of the field, too. Unable to cry out for being choked with churned earth, turning over and over against the curved blades of the plough arm while his blood spilled into the soil, souring it with his death. That's what drew the corpse-wort, they say. The bloodweed. Land's been cursed ever since.'

Leese brought a shirt to her mother and ladled her a bowl of the broth. It seemed to Rutger that the story was finished, but just as he spooned up the last of his own supper, Maudeline spoke again.

'The wife was ruined with grief. She took sick and fell beyond the healing powers of her husband, succumbing to her suffering. The husband, already hollowed with one loss, slaughtered the ox in a fit of grief-borne rage. His neighbours, they were unable or unwilling to help him after, and though they pitied him, they did little to stop his crops failing and provided nothing from their own harvest. When he, too, grew sick, the Great Necromancer came for him.'

'Nagash,' Leese whispered. Maudeline hushed her, but nodded.

'The Great Necromancer prevented the man's death, prolonging his grief as punishment for those he'd managed to save when he was a healer, those he'd denied the necromancer over the years. And with eternity, the poor man's grief manifested into anger. His disgust for those who'd failed to help him and his wife turned to fury until all he had was hate and resentment. It drove him to take up the curved tines of the plough, the sickle, the scythe, whatever he could find, and he took his revenge on all who lacked the compassion he'd once held so dear. Over the years, people learned to make gifts to appease him or keep him at bay. These are the tributes that became reaping gifts, so that other neighbours would not suffer the same fate or fall at the hands of the Reaperman.'

Maudeline pushed her bowl of broth to Rutger. She'd barely touched it and nodded for him to eat. 'You've never heard that story?'

'Something like it,' he said, and took the offered bowl. 'Thank you.'

Maudeline shrugged. 'There's a different Reaperman for every farmstead, probably. Stories are a way of reminding ourselves we're a community, which can be easy to forget out here, divided by fields and fences.'

'And are there many of you in this community?' Rutger asked.

'Not as many as there were.'

'The Reaperman came for them,' Poll said.

'Some of them, maybe,' Maudeline said. 'Others went to war. Likely the same war you're running from.'

Rutger looked away.

'It's all right,' Maudeline said. 'You'll find no judgement here. I only wish my husband would do the same.'

The look she gave Rutger made him feel wanted and hated at the same time. That he could have been her husband, but was not.

'Don't wish for that,' Rutger said. 'They hang deserters.' It made him remember the man o' straw hanging in the barn, roped and limp against the wall.

'Better to risk the rope than get split across the middle. What good could he be to us with his belly open and his guts streaming out?'

Maudeline was turning the shirt that Leese had given her in her hands. For a moment Rutger thought it was his own, somehow washed clean and repaired; it was the same design, same colour, same cloth. Her husband's, then. But no, if he was away fighting, this was not his uniform.

The realisation came as sudden as pain and when he looked back at Maudeline he knew she'd seen it.

'You're not the first soldier to pass through this way,' she said quietly.

Rutger remembered all of the clothes the girl had taken and returned to the trunk. There had been a pile of them. How many had been uniforms?

'You can stay in the barn,' Maudeline said, reducing the shirt in her hands to strips.

To Rutger's ears, each tear sounded like a scythe cutting through corn.

With his stomach so tightly bound some of the pain had been subdued, but he still leaned on Maudeline and the lantern staff she had given him. The candle stub gave only slight light, but in the almost absolute dark of the yard it was enough to guide them.

'It's hard, surviving out here.'

Rutger said nothing.

'The army visited every homestead, every farm they passed through, rounding up the able-bodied. Including my husband. They said he had to go and I said he had to stay and you can see who won that battle. They took our old mule, too, though it weren't much good for anything but its manure any more, and all of our chickens save one. If it wasn't for those three in there, I'd have been pressed into service, too. Still, it taught me an important lesson.'

'What's that?'

'Take what you can from those who have it.'

Rutger grunted. 'Not all deserters get the rope,' he said.

'Not if they come through this way.'

Rutger stopped. He moved away from Maudeline and leaned against a water pump. 'Why bother sewing me up? Why feed me?' He was looking at the sword she wore; before leaving the house, she had retrieved it from the trunk – one weapon from a choice of several – and made a show of fastening it around her waist.

Maudeline had no answer for his question. Nothing she was willing to give, anyway.

'Do I remind you of him?'

She took his arm and pulled him towards the barn. 'No, you do not.'

'Then why? If I'm only going to become a pile of clothes and belongings, why waste your food and thread?'

She sighed. 'The meat's ruined.'

'The meat?'

'It's festering. Infected. I can't tell quite what. Perhaps the weapon that ripped you open was poisoned with something. All I know is I wouldn't trust it for my children.'

Rutger pulled away again, though without the pump to lean on he wasn't very steady on his feet. 'Sigmar's mercy.' He was grateful his broth had only been vegetable water.

'I suppose you could call it that.' She met his look without flinching. 'You've seen the wasted state of the crops. Blood-weed isn't fit for eating, and the crows are no better. We get eggs from our one scrawny chicken, but so rarely that I'd cook it if it weren't all beak, bone and feathers.'

Rutger could barely look at her. How many had come this way, only to find themselves meat in her larder?

'You can sleep safe tonight,' Maudeline told him, 'and then be on your way elsewhere tomorrow. Anything I might have taken from you, I'd have taken already.'

Rutger was still looking at the sword. She was right; he was in no fit state to fight her. He hung his head in resignation.

That was when he saw it.

'Maudeline. Look.'

Warily, she looked to where he pointed and saw the churned mud. The night sky was cloudy, almost lightless, but Rutger lowered the lantern towards the ground to reveal a number of split-hoof prints. They circled the chicken coop. Maudeline began to follow them.

'I heard something out here earlier,' she said. 'An animal.' She eased the sword she wore from its sheath and held it point forward, ready to lunge.

'No,' Rutger said, 'wait,' and stepped forward to restrain her.

It came out of the darkness with surprising speed. They saw it only briefly by the weak light of the candle stub, but it was enough to frighten them into a shared gasp. Its face was long like that of a horse, but more like a goat's in shape and features, with long horns curling back from its head. It snarled at them, teeth jagged and sharp, and raised a hairy fist to show a cleaver-like weapon. Rutger noted the beast's lack of armour, saw only a strap of leather across the pelt of its own chest and a tattered loincloth at its groin, and then Maudeline was in his way. She slashed her blade across the creature's chest, stepping in close to avoid its own weapon as she brought hers up again with sudden speed. Rutger saw it sink into the beast's armpit and then the two of them toppled away into the dark.

For a moment he stood rooted, a statue unable to act. But a guttural cry called him to action and he hurried forward.

The two were writhing on the ground. Rutger saw the cleaver abandoned and kicked it away, yelling at the strain it put on his wound. The beast was clawing at Maudeline, turning her clothes to bloody tatters, but she held her position atop it, forearm pressed to its throat and her other stabbing again and again at whatever part of it she could find with her weapon. Rutger jabbed at the creature's face with the shaft of the lantern pole but it was knocked away in the fray. In his fumble to keep hold of it he managed to reverse it around and brought it down with both hands, hard, smashing the lantern into the beast's head just as Maudeline slammed her sword up under its chin, pinning its jaw closed.

The rest was done in darkness. Rutger held back, not wanting to strike Maudeline, but he heard the grunts and breaths of their struggle. It was brief. Once his eyes grew accustomed to the night, he saw Maudeline sit back, still astride the creature, sword dripping in her fist. She was soaked with blood and smeared with mud, little more than a pale face in the darkness, panting and fierce.

Rutger toed the beastman's shoulder, turning the body

slightly to show a crushed quiver of arrows beneath it, a broken bow once slung on its back now held together only by its string.

'It's a scout.'

'How many?' Maudeline asked. She tried to stand, staggered, and was helped up by Rutger. 'Are there more?'

'I don't know. We should go.'

'Go where?'

'Anywhere. A neighbour? And then another neighbour, and so on.'

'We have none.'

'None?'

'Not nearby, anyway.' She swept her hair back from her face. It stayed in place, slick with blood and mud and rainwater. She looked at Rutger. 'Not all the clothes in that trunk are uniforms.'

She was daring his judgement; all he could do was look away.

'This one will be missed,' he said, gesturing at the fallen beast. 'Its absence will be its report and a warband will come.'

She pointed her sword at him. 'They're looking for you.'

Rutger stepped back. 'Battle's moving this way,' he said. 'They're looking for anyone.'

For a moment, brief as a star falling, Rutger saw all the fight and fierceness leave her. The strength abandoned her limbs and the blade hung limp in her hand. 'They'll cut right through this place,' she said.

'We have to run.'

'They'll catch us.'

They would. Unless there was something to hold them here a while.

Rutger looked towards the barn. 'I have an idea.'

'Great. What we need is an army.'

Rutger agreed, and he told her some of his plan.

The sun remained hidden for now, but some of its light was leaking into the sky and a brightening amethyst jewelled the ridge of the farm. The rain had stopped and the wet stalks of corn seemed to shine with the morning. Rutger, pausing for breath, held his stomach and looked back at the ruse they'd constructed.

It hadn't taken long to ready the farm, not with the family helping. Every man o' straw had been fetched from the barn and new ones had been hastily made using the clothes from the trunk. Using some repurposed fencing, each had been strategically planted around the property, some under Rutger's guidance and the rest by Rutger himself. He'd needed their help initially – without Harren clambering up to the roof, there was no way Rutger could have positioned the man o' straw at the chimney, a curve of wagon wheel held like a bow in its handless grip – but once the more difficult jobs had been completed, Rutger had been able to manage the rest alone.

Standing close, in the yard, the full foolishness of the trick was clear, but from this distant field, looking back, Rutger thought the scarecrows would be convincing enough to warrant pause, especially those dressed in uniforms. The purpose was merely to buy some time. A full warband in the heat of battle-lust would simply pour down upon the farm regardless, of course, but a cautious warband or scouting party would linger to plan their approach and attack.

At least, that was what Rutger hoped.

'This is senseless,' Maudeline had said. 'The time we're spending with this distraction is time wasted. We should be leaving.'

'At night?'

'I can find our way in the dark.'

'I've no doubt, but you'd be a fool to try. If a party discovers this place abandoned, they'll move right on through Mhurghast and find you before the sun has fully risen. They move faster than you.'

'The Gowers have a horse.'

Rutger looked at her then, considering this news.

'She's a tired old mare, but–'

'If she could be so easily taken, you'd have done so already, if only for food. My guess is that the Gowers have learnt about your visits to other neighbours, or are otherwise too many, too strong, or too wily to be easily plundered.'

He took her silence as agreement.

Poll had been breaking boards into shield shapes. He'd proven a resourceful boy; the stuffed archer on the roof had been his idea. 'It's like your shadows,' he'd said, and put his hands together to mimic a flapping bird.

'Children's games,' Maudeline had muttered.

Leese, picking up on her mother's mood, had pointed out, 'They won't be very convincing if they can't move.'

'Then we'll make them move.'

'How?'

'The same way your weathervane works.'

Maudeline had looked up at the roof, though it was too dark to see anything. 'And if there's no wind?'

As it turned out, her concern had been warranted. This morning, with the rain clouds dispersed, the dawn was calm. Barely any breeze rustled the corn. But it didn't matter, not now.

Rutger leaned forward, as much as his wound allowed, and tried to catch his breath. He was already exhausted.

'We won't be able to wait for you,' Maudeline had warned him.

'I know. It doesn't matter.'

She'd handed him one of the swords from the trunk. Each of her children had strapped one on as well. Rutger made a few practised swings. The sword was fine, but his movement was not.

'The only gift I have to give you is time,' he'd said. To emphasise his point, he moved his arm away from where he cradled his stomach; a dark line had soaked through to the linen of his borrowed shirt. 'I think I'll rest here a while.'

Maudeline, practical, had nodded. 'Soldiers,' she'd said. 'Always giving their lives away.'

In that moment, Rutger had felt every bit the hero he'd always wanted to be, but knew he was not.

Now, as he waited a moment for the sun to rise, Rutger remembered the story she'd told at supper. It reminded him of the Harridan Curse, and he wondered if the Reaperman was merely a farmer's version of the awful Dreadscythe. If he remembered the tale correctly, it was blood and injury that drew the Dreadscythe Harridans, though no longer from any lingering memory of their prior lives as healers but rather as creatures that delighted in causing such suffering. As a boy, he had thought it terrible that a person's character could be so corrupted, but as he grew into an adult he recognised its truth in the world. Now he thought the worst thing about the story was the idea that some inkling of what they used to be remained inside their new cursed form so that even as they attacked the living, some part of them screamed in powerless torment against what they had become.

Rutger understood that, too, and though a purer part of him rebelled against what he intended to do, he'd long ago learnt that nature was difficult to tame. His mettle had been formed in the forge of war, and there was no changing the shape of it now. Even if he could, these people had taught him something else…

Take what you can from those who have it. Do whatever it takes to survive.

He'd subdued the woman, first.

As a farrier's boy, he was familiar with how to approach a horse that might kick, just as he knew how to swing a hammer hard and true. As she'd filled a sack with meagre provisions – 'I could pack all we have and we'd still be travelling light' – Rutger had retrieved a hatchet from the woodpile and brought the back of it down hard across the back of her skull.

After her, the children had been easy.

He could still just about see where the eldest of the children, Harren, struggled against the ropes binding him to the stake in the farmyard. Arms bound outstretched as if waiting to fight, he pivoted left and right. A distance away, with several scarecrows between them, his sister's struggles had the same effect, and further away still was Poll. Their movements only served to make the ploy more convincing to whatever might see them from afar.

'I'm sorry,' Rutger muttered, though he doubted his own words.

He looked again to where his wound was suppurating unseen beneath his bandages and remembered Maudeline's opinion of it, that he was poisoned or infected. Perhaps she was right. Perhaps he would not endure the wound for long, but he would try. That was the lesson he had taken from this family's survival, though it was a lesson Maudeline hadn't meant to give.

He'd bound her in the house, too weak to position her with the others. He wondered if she was conscious yet and thought it perhaps better if she were not.

They would have died anyway, he told himself, shrugging the sack of stolen supplies into a more comfortable position over his shoulder. Out here, a woman and three children, fleeing from such beasts? They had no chance.

Such was the flimsy argument he made for himself, believing it about as much as he believed his apology for the part he'd play in their demise. But this way, at least they would provide a little more time for Rutger to reach the family with the horse. How he would fare from there, he did not know, but he would forge forward until such a time.

He stood for a moment, bathing in the light of a new dawn, and raised his arms to either side as if he, too, were some man o' straw standing in a stubbled field, corn stalks whispering at his back. And with his arms open, he welcomed the crows circling the farm. He had startled them once, shaken them from where they pecked at morsels in the field to burst black and panicked into the sky. Now they waited to feed again, eager to peck at what had once been a battlefield, to take what they could from whatever they found there.

'I'm sorry,' he said again, meaning it no more than he had the first time. 'But thank you.'

In the moment before he turned away, he heard the wind rustle through the corn behind him. He heard the quiet, drawn out hush of whispering stalks, and somewhere within that sound was the unmistakable shush of a scythe slicing through crops. A reaping sound.

He felt it come like a dying breath, and it was as if the wind passed through his own body. As if he himself was made of little more than straw.

Beyond the ridge came the drawn-out call of a battle horn, signalling someone's end.

YOUR
NEXT READ

GOTHGHUL HOLLOW
by Anna Stephens

The once illustrious Gothghul family endures seasons of isolation in their castle overlooking the Hollow. But when the town is threatened by a spate of sinister manifestations, they must uncover a diabolic mystery to which they have but one clue: Mhurghast.

The Wolf and the Rat

C L Werner

Beneath the display of smug arrogance, the Wolf could smell the tang of fear. There was no masking the scent, not from the lord of Ulfenkarn. Radukar let his lip curl back in the faintest hint of a smile, one pearly fang glistening in the flickering candlelight.

There was a moment where Radukar could see the confidence in the speaker's attitude falter. His voice caught, and from the base of the dais the messenger's eyes darted to the guards positioned either side of the Wolf's throne. Though they stood at the foot of the steps, their brutish heads were on the same level as that of their seated master. Kosargi Nightguard – vicious ogors who'd served Radukar in life and continued to obey his every command in undeath. Even to a vampire they were an imposing sight, and a formidable menace.

'These terms are generous,' the messenger said.

Radukar tapped one of his clawed fingers against the arm of his throne, digging his nail into the wood and letting the splinters scatter to the floor. The chair had been carved for a prince of the ven Altens from shadeoak, one of the toughest woods known in Shyish, and this reminder that the ogors were far from the most fearsome thing in the Ebon Citadel seemed not to go unnoticed by the messenger. The vampire's flesh was already pale, and it was impossible for the undead to sweat, but Radukar could smell the fear crawling through the messenger's gut like an infestation of maggots.

'We only want what is our right,' the messenger said, making a show of assuming a bold posture, as though such theatrics could deceive the Wolf.

'Valac Chrobak.' Radukar let the name hiss from between his fangs. 'What do you expect to gain from this? What is to be your reward?'

'The governing council will be re-established,' Valac said.

'And Kritza has told you that you will sit on this council?' The question came in a low growl.

All pretence of Valac's bravado was suddenly extinguished, and he waved his arms in a placating gesture. 'There is a place for you on the council...'

Radukar leaned forwards, his crimson eyes boring down into the other vampire. 'Is that so? I am to be *permitted* to share power, am I? A council of equals, is it?' He barked with cruel laughter. 'You will sit at the table as my equal, Valac Chrobak? Were you not a traitor I would appoint you as my jester. You have a flair for the absurd.'

The doors at the far end of the hall swung open as the mouldering servitors admitted a tall, broad-shouldered woman dressed in black. Natasyia's red hair was pulled back into a single braid, which draped over her shoulder, weighted down by a ruby that glistened like blood. Her complexion had a milky paleness to it, somehow more graceful than the sickly hue of Valac's. She barely gave the messenger a glance as she approached the throne, then dropped to one knee before Radukar and bowed her head.

'It is as this glib scallywag says, milord,' Natasyia declared, her words twisted by the piratical jargon of her old life. Before becoming seneschal of the Ebon Citadel and receiving the Blood Kiss, she'd been the most notorious corsair to prowl the waters of Banshee's Bay. Radukar's intervention had kept the princes of Mournhold from hanging her. Now, with the city reborn as Ulfenkarn under the Wolf's rule, Natasyia enjoyed power far surpassing that of a mere pirate captain. 'This scug or his friends got into the vaults and took the pelt.' She turned a withering glance at Valac.

Radukar rose from his seat and pointed down at Valac. 'Do you know what you've taken from me?' he snarled. 'The hide of my father-in-darkness, last of the Vyrkos Blood-kings!' He splayed his fingers, curling them until his hands resembled vulturine talons. 'I peeled that skin from him after I bested him in combat and proved myself the true master of the Vyrkos! Before ever I sailed the *Impaler's Gift* to this city and rescued it from Slaughn's Chaos hordes, that pelt was my most precious treasure. A tangible reminder of my impossible victory. Evidence that my destiny is to conquer and command.'

Valac shifted uneasily, his eyes widening as he felt the Wolf's ire focused upon him. 'The hide will be returned to you. You need only meet our demands. Lord Kritza—'

A gesture from Radukar sent his Kosargi Nightguard lumbering towards Valac. 'Kritza sent you here to die. Surely you know that.'

The messenger sprang back. His weapons had been taken from him before entering the throne room, but he whipped out a dagger from some hidden pocket. Animalistic fury contorted Valac's face, but it was the desperate rage of a cornered rat, not the vicious strength of a predator. He leaped forward, but as soon as he was in motion, Natasyia struck him and threw him aside. He crashed to the floor, then turned to stare up at her with a look of horror. In the next moment, one of the Kosargi grabbed him and lifted him up by his head. As Valac struggled in the ogor's crushing grip, the other Nightguard let its halberd drop and reached into its belt to retrieve a sharpened stake. The guard rammed it into Valac's chest with a sickening impact, shattering ribs as it drove up through the vampire's heart, abruptly silencing his protestations.

'Hoist that carrion up onto the battlements,' Natasyia told the Kosargi. She scowled at Valac's corpse as the skin began to rot and peel away. 'Let that scum be a warning of the price of mutiny.'

Radukar sank back into his throne while the Nightguard carried the traitor's body away. 'So, the Rat Prince thinks to bargain for power,' he spat. 'Kritza should have been satisfied with simply being alive.' The Wolf gnashed his fangs in anger that the sly nobleman had survived destruction. When Kritza had been thrown into the corpse-cart for disposal, that should have been the end of him. Instead, he'd somehow managed to revive himself and escape. Radukar had underestimated his enemy's tenacity. It was a mistake he wouldn't make a second time.

'Valac claimed Kritza would meet with you to exchange the Vyrkos pelt for your blood-oath,' Natasyia said.

Radukar nodded. 'Kritza and his conspirators are demanding that I restore the old council – to share rule with them.' He flashed a toothy smile at his seneschal. 'I am to meet them at Grimmarrow Shipyard to sign the compact they've drawn up.'

Natasyia's lips parted in a carnivorous grin, the sort of smile she'd worn when executing prisoners back in her pirate days. 'If Kritza thinks to trap you, you can trap him instead, milord. The mutineers would likely spot the Kosargi if you brought them, but they'd have a harder time noticing the Deathrattle. I could surround the shipyard with the household guard. Even if they were spotted, they'd be mistaken for Ulfenwatch patrols.'

'See to it,' Radukar pronounced. The Wolf swiftly descended from the dais, his cloak billowing around him as he stalked from the hall. 'I am impatient to teach these traitors that no one defies me in my own city!' His voice trailed away in a lupine growl. 'Kritza will learn that there are worse things waiting for him when he's once more in my power.'

The Grimmarrow Shipyard was wreathed in darkness and decay. The hulks of half-finished vessels cast eerie shadows about the setting, the beams of their hulls looking like the bones of ancient godbeasts rotting beneath the sinister light of the Shyish Nadir. An entire fleet of stillborn whaling ships littered the place, their construction abandoned in the cataclysm that transformed bustling Mournhold into vampire-haunted Ulfenkarn. Between the dry docks, the tools and materials of the builders were strewn. The rank stink of pitch was overwhelming as neglected barrels failed and began to leak. The stench was enough to keep the area free of the blood-thirsty bats that infested most of the city, but their place was taken by slinking diregoyles and packs of mangy, half-necrotic cats. The gnawed carcass of some luckless trespasser who'd thought to find refuge in the shipyard poked out from beneath a tumbled heap of lumber – a solemn reminder that there was no safety for the living to be found here.

The undead scavengers and lurking ghouls didn't menace the white-cloaked intruder who prowled alone through their territory, however. Senses keen to the spark of mortality could likewise detect the deathly energies that emanated from the figure. Even the lowest beast in Ulfenkarn could recognise the dread aspect of the monster that ruled the city.

A dark fur cap cast Radukar's wolfish features in shadow as he marched boldly through the shipyard. The white cloak that fell from his shoulders was fashioned from the pelt of the giant, two-headed wolf Vilnas, and seemed to bristle with the vampire's smouldering rage. Radukar had killed the beast long before ever venturing to Mournhold, slaughtering the creature that guarded the tomb of the vampiric emperor, Morkan. That feat had been accomplished when Radukar had still been mortal, and had impressed the Vyrkos enough to bestow on him the Blood Kiss… and thereby ensure their own doom.

Radukar's hand fell to the sword that hung from his belt – another trophy from the Tomb of Morkan. The barrow-blade had drank deeply of vampire blood when the Wolf had turned upon the Vyrkos, slaughtering the entire tribe. Now the only Vyrkos to be found in Shyish were those he'd ushered into his Thirsting Court.

His fangs gleamed in the starlight. After this meeting with Kritza, there would be even fewer to represent the bloodline.

The audacity of the Rat Prince! To dare to steal from the master of Ulfenkarn! Whatever else happened, Radukar was determined that Kritza would regret his boldness. The traitor should have found some hole to hide in, grateful to have escaped at all. Now he squandered such miraculous good fortune by pitting himself against the Wolf once more. Radukar could almost find such tenacity admirable, if it weren't so pathetic.

The Wolf felt the presence of the other vampires before he saw them. He'd known the moment Valac had arrived at the Ebon Citadel that Kritza wouldn't meet with him alone. There were half a dozen other vampires with the Rat Prince – idiots who'd been swayed by the lure of power he had offered them. Ambition was ever the nemesis of prudence.

Radukar stopped beneath the prow of a hull with the name *Majestic Vengeance* carved across it. A theatrical touch from the self-important Kritza. This was the place. Even if he hadn't sensed the other vampires nearby, he knew the traitor's extravagance wouldn't have allowed him to overlook such a spot to make the trade.

'I know you're there,' Radukar growled. He stepped out into the gap between the *Majestic Vengeance* and the hull of the ship beside it. He wanted to show the traitors that he had no need to be cautious. They were of no threat to him. 'Return what you've stolen and I may even allow you to live.'

There was a stirring among the shadows. 'Mercy from the Usurper? I'd expect patience from a vargskyr first!'

Out from the gloom stepped Kritza. He was a tall, slender man, his features stamped with the arrogance of pampered nobility. Silken leggings and a rich double-breasted coat complemented the carefully groomed appearance. Even when hiding from Radukar's wrath, Kritza must have found some tailor to make his thrall. The other vampire moved with a skittering step, guiding himself with a gilded walking stick fitted with an orb of bloodstone at its top. He stopped a few yards from the *Majestic Vengeance* and made a sideways gesture with his cane. His retinue crept out from the dark, all of them arrayed in the extravagant finery of Mournhold's old nobility.

'You've bragged to the dragon about stealing from his hoard,' Radukar said. His gaze swept across Kritza and his companions. Only the Rat Prince was able to meet the Wolf's fiery eyes; the others flinched and shrank back. 'Do you expect to survive this foolishness?'

Kritza's face pulled back in a sneer, the same expression of disdain the mortal nobles had shown Radukar before he had brought their city crashing into ruins. With a flourish, the Rat Prince reached beneath his coat and brought forth the desiccated hide of the last Vyrkos Blood-king – Radukar's sire-in-darkness. 'I have this, and if you want it back you will agree to my terms.' He looked aside at the other conspirators. '*Our* terms,' he corrected himself. 'We know how precious this relic is to you. That you'd do anything to have it safely back in your possession.' He brandished the pelt as though waving a rag before a bullgor in the arena. 'Something to recall to your past triumphs? So you don't forget your victory over the Vyrkos?' He shook his head. 'Sentimentality is the bane of peasants. It is why the low-born are unfit to rule. A red-handed pirate has his uses, but he really must remember his place.'

Radukar's lips curled back from his fangs. 'If the princes of Mournhold had been competent rulers, they'd never have fallen so easily into my grasp. Those born to power become ignorant to its value. They don't know what it is to hunger for it, and therefore don't appreciate it until it is stripped from them.'

'I am taking it back,' Kritza snapped. 'I am taking it all back.' He waved the pelt at Radukar again. 'Things will be as they once were. The city will be ruled by the old families and you... you will remember your place!'

'The arrogance of madness,' Radukar retorted. 'A little while ago, I considered sparing Valac to serve me as court jester, but now I realise that you're a far greater fool than he could ever have been.' The Wolf shifted his attention away from Kritza and regarded the other vampires. 'Tell me, which of these traitors was brazen enough to steal from me? I know such direct action is beneath the presumed dignity of the Rat Prince. Tell me, Kritza, which of these idiots is a bigger fool than you?'

'None of them,' said a voice behind him. The Wolf turned and watched as Natasyia emerged from the shadows. In her wake came a dozen armoured skeletons, halberds and spears gripped in their fleshless hands. All around the shipyard, other Ulfenwatch soldiers silently shuffled into position, forming a cordon around the scene. A single glance at the hate in his seneschal's face told Radukar that the traitor within the Ebon Citadel was the former pirate lord.

'So, you stole the pelt from me,' Radukar growled. 'Was it your idea or his to throw everything away for such recklessness?'

Natasyia circled around Radukar, her eyes boring into him. 'You promised me power, Radukar, but you didn't warn me of the price I'd have to pay!' Her hand closed around a beam protruding from an unfinished hull. Under the pressure of her fingers, the pitch-coated wood exploded into splinters. 'Strength to match a cryptkraken! The swiftness of a deepmare! The keenness of a tide tiger! All these things you promised!'

'And you have them,' Radukar rebuffed her.

The seneschal glowered at him. 'I have them, but there's no pleasure to be derived from such power! No satisfaction! You didn't warn me that everything would feel hollow, that there'd be no joy or excitement, only the futile chase for sensation. Anything to make me feel...'

Radukar laughed at her agony. 'Alive? You want to feel alive again, little pirate? That is the one thing you can never have. You've taken the Blood Kiss and there's no going back. Whatever you do to betray me, you will always be my creature.'

Natasyia made to leap for Radukar, but Kritza held his stick out to block her path. His eyes glittered with verminous cunning. 'Don't let him goad you,' he warned her. 'I made that mistake once. Never again.' Kritza smiled and pointed to the cordon of skeletons. 'Don't you see it is the Usurper who's made the mistake? The pelt drew him to us, and now you've brought your troops to keep him from escaping.'

A withering smile shaped itself across Natasyia's face as she glared at Radukar.

Kritza's retinue jeered as the Ulfenwatch closed in.

'You thought we would share power with you again, Usurper?' the Rat Prince mocked. 'To return to the system you used to steal our city from us? There will be no compact, Radukar, no place in the new order for you.'

A nod from Kritza and his conspirators drew their blades. One of the vampires broke away from the group. Dashing between the ships, he retrieved an oil lamp from where it had been hidden inside a box of tools. He thumbed open its catch, spurring it into full flame. An overhand swing sent it crashing against the *Majestic Vengeance*, followed by a loud whoosh as the skeletal ship ignited. The beams had been slathered with pitch and the fire swiftly spread, building towards a roaring conflagration.

Radukar edged away from the burning hull, glaring defiantly at Kritza and Natasyia. He slowly drew his sword as the other vampires surrounded him. A spectral chill emanated from the corroded barrow-blade. 'Which of you will be first to cross swords with your master?' Radukar snarled.

'We aren't here to fight you,' Kritza sneered. He waved his fellow conspirators back before the Vyrkos taint provoked them into action. 'We're here to watch you burn.' He pointed his stick at the blazing ship. 'That is to be your pyre, Usurper!'

Natasyia gestured to the armoured skeletons. 'Push him back into the fire!' she commanded. The Ulfenwatch lowered their spears and slowly converged on Radukar.

The Wolf barked with laughter. 'You're to be congratulated, Kritza! Bringing your entire rotten conspiracy to one place! You've saved me from ferreting the traitors from their holes.' He scowled at Natasyia. 'I knew you were bold enough to defy me, but I didn't think you were stupid enough to do so!'

The seneschal gnashed her fangs in fury, but didn't let her savagery overwhelm her.

The Ulfenwatch continued their slow march. Radukar made no move to escape, nor did he even adopt a defensive pose as they came closer. Instead he simply laughed.

'Did you really think I would place that much trust in you?' he said, his voice dripping with scorn. 'Did you think I'd leave any possibility that you could use my own guards against me? You should have paid more attention, Natasyia, before joining Kritza's intrigues!' Radukar waved his hand in an arcane gesture before the marching skeletons. The Ulfenwatch fell still at once, each one frozen in place by the Wolf's unspoken command.

'Kill him!' Natasyia shouted, but the skeletons ignored her order.

'Before we left the Ebon Citadel, I took the precaution of exerting my own will over the guards,' Radukar said, 'in case you took it in mind to use them against me.'

'This changes nothing!' Kritza declared, though it was clear from his expression he was unsettled by Radukar's anticipation of their scheme. He composed himself once more, then nodded to Natasyia. 'We've still drawn him away from his castle. He's within our grasp!' The Rat Prince gestured to the other vampires. 'Kill the Usurper and the city belongs to us!'

The vampires took up Kritza's cry. They charged Radukar en masse, their vicious Vyrkos blood driving them into a frenzy. They threw aside the unmoving skeletons that stood in their way before launching themselves at the Wolf.

Radukar met the traitors with his own assault. Flinging himself forwards, he whipped his barrow-blade out in a scything arc. One of the vampires was struck mid-leap, her body cleft in half by the Wolf's sword. She hissed up at him from the ground, but his stamping boot crushed her skull before she could sink her fangs into his heel.

A second sought to parry the sweep of Radukar's sword with his own blade, but the Wolf's corroded steel proved far stronger than that of his adversary. It sheared through the lesser weapon as though it were paper and continued on to sever the arm that held it. The mutilated vampire recoiled and clutched at his wound. Radukar was on him at once, seizing him by the neck and drawing him close. Blood sprayed across the Wolf's twin-headed cloak as his fangs ripped out the other vampire's throat. He tossed the mutilated corpse aside as though it were an old rag.

Radukar wiped his gore-stained mouth with the back of his hand. 'Which of you fools is next?'

The Wolf's challenge echoed through the shipyard. Standing before the blazing hulk of the *Majestic Vengeance*, with the bodies of two slaughtered foes at his feet, Radukar presented an imposing sight; too imposing for the traitors Kritza had gathered into his conspiracy. What had been a ferocious assault a moment before had now degenerated into a rout as the vampires turned and fled.

Radukar exerted his monstrous will, denying the predatory instinct that compelled him to give chase to his enemies. There was no need to pursue them, and howls of frustrated despair rang out as the vampires discovered there was no escape. The Wolf grinned, picturing their surprise as they ran straight into his waiting Kosargi Nightguard.

Two figures came slinking back towards the burning *Majestic Vengeance*. Kritza bore a frantic aspect that reminded Radukar of an admiral he'd once done battle with off the coast of Necros. The *Impaler's Gift* had lured a fleet of galleys into the shoals, smashing them to pieces upon the rocks. The Wolf had never forgotten the admiral's face as he unwittingly led his ships into the trap – the face of a man who was realising too late the magnitude of the mistake he'd made.

Natasyia had returned with the Rat Prince, her cutlass in one hand, its blade reflecting the flames from the still burning ship. The swaggering confidence from before had left her. Like Kritza, she'd assumed the look of a hunted thing. Better than the rest of the conspirators, she knew the awesome power of Radukar's ogors.

'You brought your bodyguards,' Natasyia cursed. 'Even while I was deploying the Ulfenwatch to trap you.'

'You were too eager to put your scheme into action,' Radukar told her. 'Too intent on your plan. You should have noticed the Kosargi following us. Treachery is crime enough, but incompetence is unforgivable.'

Natasyia spun around, exhibiting the supernatural speed bestowed on her by the Blood Kiss. Before Kritza could react, she snatched the Vyrkos pelt from his hand. She shook it at Radukar as though it were a captured flag. 'I still have this,' she snarled. Her eyes darted from side to side as the Kosargi lumbered towards them out of the darkness. Each carried a massive stake of sharpened bloodthorn, the bodies of treacherous vampires spitted upon their cruel shafts.

The faithless seneschal dashed past the advancing ogors to reach the blazing form of the *Majestic Vengeance*. She held the pelt close to the snarling flames. 'Call them off, Radukar,' she demanded. 'Send them away or your precious treasure burns!'

Kritza crowed with pleasure at the sudden turnabout. 'Sentimentality, Usurper,' he laughed, his face bearing a defiant look once more. 'We still hold power over you. You'll do as we say or pay the price!'

The Wolf glowered at the Rat Prince. 'If you were wise, you'd have fled Ulfenkarn while you had the chance. But seldom is arrogance married to wisdom. I've prepared a special stake for you on the Ebon Citadel's battlements. It overlooks the ruins of your old palace. An appropriate view for you to look upon as your own weight drags you down and your heart is slowly skewered.' Radukar smiled at the fright that shone in Kritza's eyes as he described the vampire's fate. He shifted his attention to Natasyia. 'You've been a great disappointment to me. I bestowed the gifts of the Vyrkos on you, made you my seneschal, because I thought you were not unlike me. You described all the mortal sensations that you've lost, but not the one that burns brighter than before – the thrill of the hunt, Natasyia! How can any mortal experience compare to that which we now know! Yet you failed to appreciate this, and instead threw your lot in with preening nobles like Kritza!'

'Stay back!' Natasyia warned as Radukar started towards her. She waved the Vyrkos pelt at him. 'Stay back or it burns!'

Radukar stopped and fixed her with his gaze. 'Even now, you don't understand. When you received the Blood Kiss you became my creature, and my creature you still remain.' The Wolf exerted his fearsome will. Horror twisted Natasyia's face as she ceased to flourish the pelt and fell still, her body becoming rigid as she responded to Radukar's mental command.

'The scheme you hatched was audacious,' Radukar said. 'Sentimentality *is* a weakness you've exposed, Kritza,' he said. 'One that I now rid myself of.' His eyes bored into Natasyia's and the Wolf's visage curled into a mask of bestial fury. He snarled a single word: '*Burn!*'

Natasyia's eyes went wide with terror as her body responded to Radukar's order. She tried to resist as she moved towards the dancing flames, and for an instant managed to drag her foot back, but against the Wolf's power she was ultimately helpless. Step by ghastly step, she moved towards the fire-wrapt hull, the pelt clenched in her tightened fist. Smoke emanated from her body as the heat washed over her. Then her hair and clothes ignited. Natasyia howled in agony but continued to step into the blaze, incapable of breaking free of Radukar's will.

The Wolf continued to watch until Natasyia was engulfed in flames. He felt a deep bitterness watching the precious pelt she carried being consumed along with her. It had been a treasured memento from his past, but it had also become a hazard to his rule and his ambition. Destroyed, it could never again be used against him by his enemies.

'Your schemes have gone up in smoke. Now you go to join my disloyal seneschal,' Radukar growled, swinging around to face Kritza. He exerted his fearsome will upon the other vampire, but his brow knotted in surprise when the Rat Prince didn't respond to his command. Kritza remained where he was, the oily smile working itself back onto his face.

'You've no hold over me,' Kritza smirked. 'You relinquished that power when you threw me aside and left me to die.' He leaned on his walking stick, his eyes glittering with a crimson light. 'I'm not one of your Vyrkos whelps any more. I've become something else. Something beyond your control.'

Radukar flashed his fangs at Kritza. 'Then I'll leave it to my Kosargi to dispose of you,' he hissed. A gesture from the Wolf brought the undead ogors converging upon Kritza.

Before the Nightguard could reach him, a sudden transformation came over the Rat Prince. The walking stick clattered to the ground as the hands that held it evaporated. Where moments before a noble had stood, there was now a mass of writhing brown fur in his place. The Rat Prince had become a swarm of gaunt, hideous rodents.

The shape disintegrated into dozens of bodies that spilled to the ground. The squealing rats scattered in every direction, skittering between the hulking Kosargi, too small and swift to be stopped by the ogors.

Radukar sprang forwards and seized one of the vermin before it could escape, but the lone rat dissipated into a puff of greasy mist. He wiped the foul residue on his cloak. 'An interesting trick, Kritza,' he hissed. 'But when our paths cross again, I'll be ready for it.'

Radukar walked past the *Majestic Vengeance* as he made his way out of the shipyard, his Kosargi falling into step behind him. The conflagration had spread to other hulls now, and alarm bells rang out in Ulfenkarn's slums. Soon the mortal inhabitants would rush to the scene to try to contain the flames and keep them from reaching their own slovenly hovels. Radukar could almost smell their mounting fear on the wind.

The Wolf paused and cast a last look back at the inferno. He thought of the treasure he'd sacrificed, then his mind turned to the verminous Kritza. Perhaps after their next encounter Radukar would have a new pelt to replace the one he'd lost.

Whatever hole he concealed himself in, however dark his hiding place, as long as Kritza remained in Ulfenkarn the Wolf would track him down. There was only one lord of the Cursed City, and he'd tolerate no pretenders to his throne.

YOUR
NEXT READ

CURSED CITY
by C L Werner

When a series of vicious murders rock the vampire-ruled city of Ulfenkarn, an unlikely group of heroes – a vampire hunter, a vigilante, a wizard, and a soldier – must discover the truth even as the city's dread ruler takes to the streets and the bloodletting increases.

ABOUT THE AUTHORS

Mike Brooks is a science fiction and fantasy author who lives in Nottingham, UK. His work for Black Library includes the Horus Heresy Primarchs novel *Alpharius: Head of the Hydra*, the Warhammer 40,000 novels *Rites of Passage* and *Brutal Kunnin*, the Necromunda novel *Road to Redemption* and the novella *Wanted: Dead*, and various short stories. When not writing, he plays guitar and sings in a punk band, and DJs wherever anyone will tolerate him.

Ray Cluley is a British Fantasy Award winning horror writer. His short fiction has been printed and reprinted in various venues and has been translated into French, Chinese, Hungarian, and Russian. He currently lives and works in Wales.

Marc Collins is a speculative fiction author living and working in Glasgow, Scotland. He is the writer of the Warhammer Crime novel *Grim Repast*, as well as the short story 'Cold Cases', which featured in the anthology *No Good Men*. For Warhammer 40,000 he has written a number of short stories, including 'Duty Unto Death', 'The Crueltymaker's Kingdom' and 'The Death of the Prophet'. When not dreaming of the far future he works in Pathology with the NHS.

Guy Haley is the author of the Siege of Terra novel *The Lost and the Damned*, as well as the Horus Heresy novels *Titandeath*, *Wolfsbane* and *Pharos*, and the Primarchs novels *Konrad Curze: The Night Haunter*, *Corax: Lord of Shadows* and *Perturabo: The Hammer of Olympia*. He has also written many Warhammer 40,000 novels, including the first book in the Dawn of Fire series, *Avenging Son*, as well as *Belisarius Cawl: The Great Work*, *Dark Imperium*, *Dark Imperium: Plague War*, *The Devastation of Baal*, *Dante*, *Darkness in the Blood* and *Astorath: Angel of Mercy*. He has also written stories set in the Age of Sigmar, included in *War Storm*, *Ghal Maraz* and *Call of Archaon*. He lives in Yorkshire with his wife and son.

C L Werner's Black Library credits include the Age of Sigmar novels *Overlords of the Iron Dragon*, *Profit's Ruin*, *The Tainted Heart* and *Beastgrave*, the novella *Scion of the Storm* in *Hammers of Sigmar*, and the Warhammer Horror novel *Castle of Blood*. For Warhammer he has written the novels *Deathblade*, *Mathias Thulmann: Witch Hunter*, *Runefang* and *Brunner the Bounty Hunter*, the Thanquol and Boneripper series and Warhammer Chronicles: The Black Plague series. For Warhammer 40,000 he has written the Space Marine Battles novel *The Siege of Castellax*. Currently living in the American Southwest, he continues to write stories of mayhem and madness set in the Warhammer worlds.